The Hero-King Inglis is reborn as a beautiful girl who at age five cares for her childhood friend, Rafinha, as if she were the granddaughter she'd never had. ...life, she hopes to become a knight and to master the blade.

"Waah... Chris..."

"Are you okay, Rani? Here, upsy-daisy!"

**Rafinha**
(Rani)
Inglis's childhood friend and the duke's daughter. She loves Inglis and her big brother, Rafael.

1

Author: Hayaken
Illustrator: Nagu

**Reborn to Master the Blade:**
From Hero-King to Extraordinary Squire ♀

Inglis, now twelve years old, meets a holy knight and a hieral menace at a banquet.

"C'mon. I brought guests. I'd like you to meet these two."

# Eris

A special type of Artifact known as a hieral menace. Normally, she takes on the appearance of a young woman, but she can transform into a weapon at will.

"Don't worry about me."

# Leon

A young holy knight and Eris's partner. He is easygoing, candid, and friendly to Inglis and Rafinha.

"Good evening. Are you the two young lady mercenaries I've heard so much about?"

## Cyrene

A Highlander woman and the consul of Nova. Gentle and kind, she cares deeply for the townspeople.

"G-Good evening..." both girls said.

Inglis, now fifteen, takes a job as a mercenary in a town on the way to the knights' academy.

# Reborn to Master the Blade:
## From Hero-King to Extraordinary Squire ♀

### 1

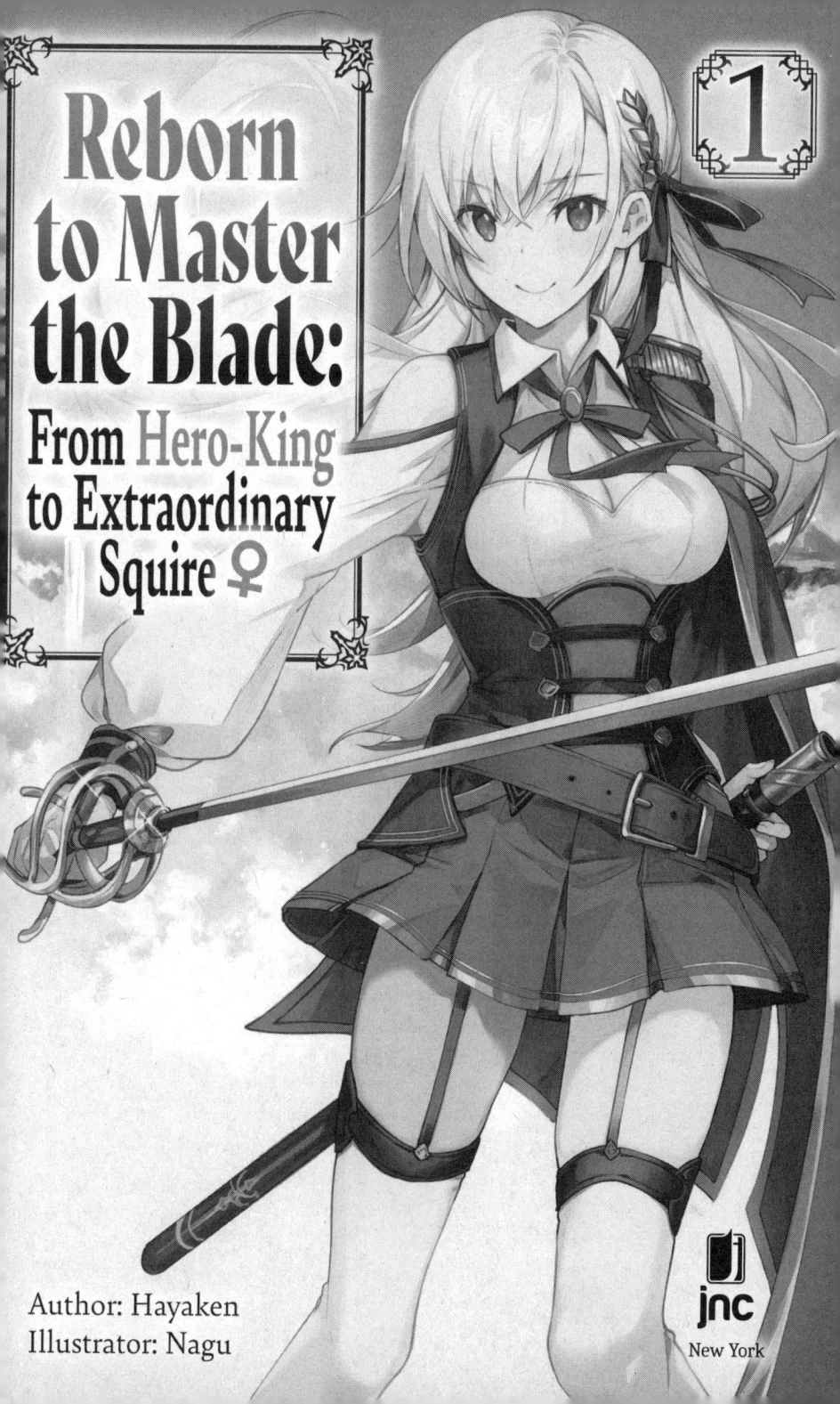

Author: Hayaken
Illustrator: Nagu

jnc
New York

# Reborn to Master the Blade:
## From Hero-King to Extraordinary Squire ♀

**1**

Author: **Hayaken**   Illustrator: **Nagu**

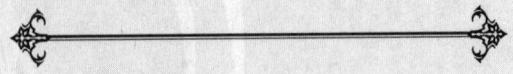

Translated by Mike Langwiser
Edited by Carly Smith

This book is a work of fiction. Names, characters, places, and incidents are the product of the author's imagination or are used fictitiously. Any resemblance to actual events, locales, or persons, living or dead, is coincidental.

EIYUOH, BU WO KIWAMERU TAME TENSEI SU.
SOSHITE, SEKAI SAIKYO NO MINARAI KISHI♀ vol. 1
© Hayaken
Illustration by Nagu
All Rights Reserved
First published in Japan by Hobby Japan Co., Ltd.
English translation rights arranged with Hobby Japan Co., Ltd. through Tuttle-Mori Agency, Inc., Tokyo

English translation © 2021 by J-Novel Club LLC

Yen Press, LLC supports the right to free expression and the value of copyright. The purpose of copyright is to encourage writers and artists to produce the creative works that enrich our culture.

The scanning, uploading, and distribution of this book without permission is a theft of the author's intellectual property. If you would like permission to use material from the book (other than for review purposes), please contact the publisher. Thank you for your support of the author's rights.

Yen Press
150 West 30th Street, 19th Floor
New York, NY 10001

Visit us at yenpress.com
facebook.com/yenpress · twitter.com/yenpress
yenpress.tumblr.com · instagram.com/yenpress

First JNC Paperback Edition: October 2023

JNC is an imprint of Yen Press, LLC.
The JNC name and logo are trademarks of J-Novel Club LLC.

The publisher is not responsible for websites (or their content) that are not owned by the publisher.

Library of Congress Cataloging-in-Publication Data is available

ISBN: 978-1-9753-7791-5 (paperback)

10 9 8 7 6 5 4 3 2 1

LSC-C

Printed in the United States of America

Reborn to Master the Blade:
From Hero-King to
Extraordinary Squire♀

# CONTENTS

Prologue: Hero-King Inglis —————————— 1

Chapter I:
Inglis, Age 0 ——————————————————— 7

Chapter II:
Inglis, Age 5 ——————————————————— 17

Chapter III:
Inglis, Age 6 ——————————————————— 31

Chapter IV:
Inglis, Age 12 (Part 1) ——————————————— 41

Chapter V:
Inglis, Age 12 (Part 2) ——————————————— 59

Chapter VI:
Inglis, Age 15—Journey to the Capital —————— 85

Chapter VII:
Inglis, Age 15—The City
Ruled by Highlanders (Part 1) ————————— 91

Chapter VIII:
Inglis, Age 15—The City
Ruled by Highlanders (Part 2) ————————— 123

Chapter IX:
Inglis, Age 15—The Rimebound Prismer ———— 149

Extra: The Talisman's Ward ——————————— 173

Afterword ————————————————————— 181

# Reborn to Master the Blade:
## From Hero-King to Extraordinary Squire ♀

# Prologue: Hero-King Inglis

In Silvaria, the capital of the Silvare Kingdom...

From a castle in the hills above looking down on his capital city, the Hero-King Inglis, founder of a continent-spanning empire, awaited his end. His attendants and retainers were huddled around his ornate deathbed, their faces bearing the nervous frowns of lost children.

And not for nothing—this aged monarch had been the bedrock of their existence. As a young man, Inglis had received the protection of the goddess Alistia, becoming a divine knight with powers beyond human limits. With those powers, he had beaten back the monsters which threatened humanity, slain the dark gods, and laid the foundations of the Silvare Kingdom. His rule was just, the fields were fertile, and his subjects smiled throughout his reign. Surely, he had built a kingdom that would last a thousand years.

Witnessing his feats and the selfless, noble spirit of his rule, the sages had confidently declared that he was the greatest king to ever live. The bards had sung hundreds, then thousands, of hymns praising him. However, now he had reached his last moments in the land he'd built. Even the greatest of heroes cannot outrun the hands of the clock, and a Silvare Kingdom without King Inglis was something none of them had ever known. No consoling words could ease their fears.

"Do not frown," King Inglis said, his tone gentle as he attempted to clear the air. "How can I rest in peace if you do not allow me to move on?" The aged king could barely lift himself from bed.

"Th-Then, get well! Your country, your people need your strength!" a retainer tearfully cried.

"If only I could. But no, this is my fate. My well-earned rest. I never could have accomplished all that I have without your aid, and I thank you for that from the depths of my heart. The future, though, is in your hands..."

His retainers continued to weep. As grateful as they were for his appreciation, it was clear his time had come. All they could do was make sure his passing came gently.

"Inglis..."

A woman's voice rang clearly in his ears. He remembered her from long ago—the only being he knew that needed no deference toward himself, whether or not he desired such a thing.

Life was strange. As a young man, he'd never even considered becoming a king. He'd thought he could live by the strength of his arms alone, but then he'd met her, and everything changed.

"It... It's been so long." The king lost his composure as a woman wrapped in glistening white robes appeared at the foot of his bed without warning.

"Your Majesty, what seems to be the matter?" a retainer asked.

Naturally, they could not see her; a god reveals their form only to humans of their choosing. As a divine knight, half-human and half-god, Inglis could see her clearly—the goddess Alistia, who had granted him her protection. She had bestowed her power unto him when he was young.

"It's nothing. Leave me for a moment. I wish to be alone," Inglis said.

His retainers filed out of the room, not a single one noticing the goddess's presence. Now, alone with her, King Inglis smiled.

"It's been so long. How many years have passed since we last met?

Yet you're as beautiful as ever. I'd hoped to see you once more before the end."

"And I as well. Inglis..." Alistia ran her hand over Inglis's wrinkled brow. "You've worked so hard. Truly. For both the world and the people in it."

"So my feeble efforts have had some merit. I suppose I've imparted something upon the ages."

"Eh heh heh. That goes for myself as well. I made no mistake in choosing you as a divine knight." Alistia smiled with otherworldly beauty after letting out a chuckle. "Inglis, I appear before you to—"

"I know. To provide me a final solace?"

"Why, of course not. After all your effort, I would reward you. What is your wish? Anything which I can grant, I will."

"Anything?"

"Yes. You've earned it through your deeds." The goddess nodded deeply, proud of him.

Inglis thought quietly for a moment, *There's no shame in the life I've lived. I should be proud of what I've accomplished, but...there's still that what-if.*

*The human spirit, a human life, contains more complexities than what a single path allows.*

King Inglis's greatest regret was never truly mastering the blade. Even as a divine knight with superhuman powers, his duties as a king had precluded even the simplest of training exercises, especially since founding the Silvare Kingdom. As a warrior, that was what he regretted most. Thus, King Inglis answered:

"Very well, then. If I've a wish, it's to be reborn."

"Why is that?"

"To live a different life. I've offered my whole self to my kingdom, my people. I have no regrets about that, only pride."

"But of course."

"But if I had lived as a warrior, rather than a king—I'm curious how far my strength would have taken me. If you'd permit me, I'd like to try living that life."

"I see. I recall you were a mercenary when we first met."

"Indeed. And deep inside, some part of me still identifies as a nameless sellsword rather than a king. May I be reborn, far enough in the future to see the fate of the land I built? To see how those come after me take up my mantle... I'd like to learn what becomes of my work here."

"I understand. Inglis, I shall grant your wish." The goddess looked upon him warmly. "I await the day, far in the future after your rebirth, when we meet again."

She embraced Inglis's frail, withered body, and he closed his eyes as he leaned into her arms. In the blink of an eye, she was gone.

As the sun slipped from the heavens that evening, so too did King Inglis from this world. His last hours were spent on his balcony, gazing at both the country he'd built and the loyal subjects he loved. Many of the citizens saw the moment the hero-king passed, his serene expression filled with beatific kindness. The Silvare Kingdom had lost its father and would trod its own path in the world without him.

Time continued its march...

He slept for what felt at once like eons yet also mere moments.

Finally, King Inglis felt his consciousness return. Through hazy vision, he looked up at two human figures, a raven-haired woman and a silver-haired man, the man hoisting Inglis aloft.

Inglis felt small, barely able to move. He was a newborn now.

*Then I truly was reborn... Divine power, indeed.*

It was certainly quite a feat.

The silver-haired man gleefully raised Inglis in the air, taking on the lilt of a proud father. "Ah ha ha ha! Inglis go whoosh, whoosh!"

The sea of ages had not yet lapped away Inglis's name. He was fine with that. After spending over a lifetime with it, he was attached to it.

"Honey, Inglis will be scared up there."

"Oh, right, sorry. Well done, though, Serena! She's just as beautiful as you!"

*What?! I'm a girl?!* Inglis tried to shout in surprise, but all that came out was a baby's "Goo-goo, ga-ga!"

# Chapter I: Inglis, Age 0

Even though Inglis had been born anew through divine powers, an infant was a delicate thing—barely able to move and exhausted within minutes when it did. Before his—no, her—first birthday, she could do nothing but live as a regular infant.

Inglis had been born into House Eucus, a minor chivalric family. Her father, Luke Eucus, was captain of the local lord's knights, and her mother, Serena, had fought in his company before retiring. Even as a baby, Inglis understood that much. She couldn't speak yet, but she could listen.

Whatever initial shock she may have felt at being reborn as a girl, the inconvenience of being so young was far more intense. Inglis had never cared much about gender anyway. How much time had passed since her past life? What had become of the hero-king's beloved Silvare Kingdom, raised by Inglis's own hand? As burning as those questions were, her inabilities to speak or even move independently were far more frustrating.

Today, Inglis's mother, Serena, had placed her in a cradle around noon. Inglis pretended to sleep while her mother, believing the child was resting, kept herself busy with household chores; these moments were Inglis's own opportunity to sneak in a little training. She would no doubt tire before long and fall asleep…

Until then, she spent that short time training.

An infant may not be able to grasp the hilt of a sword, but there were things she could do. Even as a newborn, she maintained Alistia's blessings.

She was still a divine knight, half-human and half-god, clad in the divine will... Her powers were intact, including her ability to sense not only aether but also everything that implied.

Aether was the source of all things. Everything in the world was composed of aether, differing only in nature. Even mana, the source of magic, was crystallized aether.

To weave the flow of aether, to shape the world to one's will, to control destiny itself—that was the might of the divine. It was a difficult task, far more demanding than drawing out magic from the flow of mana. It was also far more powerful. When King Inglis had received the gift of aether manipulation, in another lifetime, she had been an adult. His technique was rough, basic. It had been enough to claim the title Hero-King and to build up the Silvare Kingdom, but...

Even though her powers had been superhuman, she could only barely scrape at the door of possibility. The years rushing in had pushed away the scant hours the hero-king had wanted to use for training. As Inglis Eucus, however, she had every chance to hone her aether skills from infancy to far surpass her past life. She could perfect the path of the divine knight, to tread where even gods feared.

What would the view be from that lofty perch? She had no idea, but she would find out. She'd been given a second life to master the blade, and she wouldn't waste a single moment.

Despite her inability to move her own limbs, she could manipulate aether. Concentrating, she reached out with her mind. With the faintest touch of aether, her body floated in the air. Not bad for a newborn. Now to practice holding the effect in place...

Or so she thought, but it seemed that wasn't in the cards for today.

Panicked voices echoed in from the streets outside. "Magicite beasts! Everyone, evacuate! Get to the castle!"

## Chapter I: Inglis, Age 0

What was a magicite beast? She'd heard her parents mention them occasionally but had never actually seen one. They hadn't existed in her past life. Were they some kind of fearsome monster?

"Chris! Let's get out of— Eeek! You're... You're flying?!" her mother exclaimed as she burst into the nursery, using a nickname for the girl.

*Did she see me?!* Inglis quickly settled in her cradle and began to cry as a distraction. "Waaah! Waaah!"

"I—I must have been seeing things! Anyway, we have to get you out of here! If anything happened to you, I wouldn't be able to... Don't worry, Inglis. Mommy's here to get you somewhere safe." Taking up Inglis in her arms, Serena rushed from the house.

*Will I get to see what a magicite beast is? I'm far stronger than I was in my past life. It's a shame I haven't been able to try out my powers on something, like a fearsome monster!*

So the infant Inglis hoped, cradled in her mother's arms.

◆ ◇ ◆

As Serena fled toward the castle with Inglis, she encountered someone looking for her at the gates.

"Serena! Thank goodness, you're safe!"

"Irina! Were you waiting for me?!"

Irina was Serena's sister—in other words, Inglis's aunt. The two sisters were close, so Inglis had seen Irina often. Irina had married Duke Bilford, the lord of the Citadel of Ymir where she had been born, and was thus Duchess, and Serena had married the captain of Duke Bilford's knights.

This was Inglis's new life: she was a close relative of the duke and the daughter of the captain of his knights. It was a night-and-day difference from her previous life's birth in a lowly farming village. Regardless, she wasn't as concerned with her social status as she was with what she could make of it.

"Of course I was! I was worried!"

"But you can't leave Rafael and Rafinha alone like that! They must be so scared."

Irina had a son and a daughter, and the daughter, Rafinha, was an infant too. Inglis had met the girl many times. Was Rafinha as irked by the inconvenience of a baby's body as Inglis? If she had the mind of an adult, then surely. That was unlikely, though. Rafinha probably didn't understand what was happening.

"It's okay, Rafael is looking after Rafinha! Let's go!"

"All right!"

Serena carried Inglis into the castle. The third floor was the ducal family's private quarters, where they would be provided shelter. The robust construction of the castle was much safer than their house.

As they arrived at their destination, they saw a seven- or eight-year-old boy holding an infant waiting for them.

"Mother! You're safe!" said Rafael, Duke Bilford's eldest son and presumptive heir. He was an intelligent-looking boy with dark hair and dark eyes.

"Rafael, is Rafinha safe?"

"Yes, she's right here! She's being a good girl."

"I see. Good, then." Irina turned to Serena. "Let's wait here until the knights drive away the magicite beasts."

"As you say," Serena agreed as both mothers nodded to each other.

From her mother's arms, Inglis fixed her gaze on the scene outside. The room had a good view. From here she could see the battle on top of the walls that circled the city. There was a gigantic lizard-like monster several times larger than a human. A pair of hard, bladelike wings protruded from its back, and its forehead, neck, and back were studded with crystallized gemlike protrusions of mixed colors, ranging from red to aqua to purple. Inglis wondered if those gemlike things on its body were why it was called a magicite beast. Even from a distance, the way those gems shone implied that they were condensed mana.

There seemed to be at least ten of the lizards throughout the duchy. Warriors who must have been the knights her mother mentioned

## Chapter I: Inglis, Age 0

readied their weapons to drive the beasts back. Inglis's family watched anxiously. Their expressions were serious but not surprised. Therefore, Inglis surmised that attacks like this must occur from time to time in this new era.

*Hmm, seems like life in this age is dangerous. But I'm just fine with that.*

There seemed to be plenty of opportunity for battle. Hunting the foul, gigantic magicite beasts probably wouldn't be a bad path in life. She just had to grow up so she could give it a try.

*My hands! My hands are calling out to me! But I can't move how I want to!* Inglis screamed inside her heart, but the only sounds that could leave her mouth were "Daaa! Ga-ga-ga!"

"Chris! Calm down!" her mother exclaimed.

"It's only natural. This must be the first time she's seen a magicite beast." Irina embraced Rafinha, who was also crying. "It's no wonder she's scared."

"You're right. If only these children could live in simpler times, in a world without magicite beasts, but..."

*No, Mother! I need a foe to fight! I need to take on these magicite beasts! I need to find out what I can learn by beating them!* "Waaa!" she yowled.

"There, there, Chris. Don't be scared. Mommy will keep you safe." Serena cradled Inglis in her arms, her eyes full of a mother's love.

*No! I hate this! This is my chance, and I can't even move!*

There was another person who felt the same way.

"That's a shame. I've already gotten my Rune, yet I have to watch from here," Rafael grumbled after a pause.

This was another new development, but Inglis could tell it was likely a mark on the bodies of this era's knights. Her father, the captain of the knights, and her mother, a former knight, both carried a crest-like symbol on their dominant hand. It seemed that it was something necessary to control the weapons used to fight magicite beasts.

"Rafael, yours is a special Rune," Irina lectured. "It's the mark of those chosen to bring hope. We can't risk you now. Not until you grow into your power. You understand, right?"

So Rafael's Rune determined he would be a hero. Inglis understood well from a past life as the hero-king how tightly a hero's duty could bind, or even the duty of a noble heir. Heavy were the burdens.

"Yes, mother..." Rafael sounded taken aback by Irina's insistence. He wanted to shoulder that responsibility now; he hadn't expected to be held back.

"This should serve as a clear reminder. No matter what happens here, you need to survive. Even if it means abandoning the rest of us. Remember how important you are."

"But! Mother, I—!"

Clearly his mother didn't expect such a thing to happen today, but even the thought was hard for an earnest boy like Rafael to stomach.

That said, sometimes words take on a meaning all their own.

*Speak of the devil and he shall appear.*

*Craaasssh!*

The window of their room burst from its frame as one of the magicite beasts leaped away from the knights and toward the family's hiding place.

"Eeeek!"

Irina was sent flying by the winged lizard's impact. She shielded Rafinha in her arms but couldn't safely roll with the blow. She crashed headfirst and fell unconscious. The shock of the landing stirred Rafinha, who began to wail.

"Mother!" Rafael shouted.

"No! You need to escape!"

Serena held back Rafael's hand as he began to draw his sword before she scooped up Rafinha. She pressed both infants into Rafael's arms and took a rapier from a rack on the wall.

"I'll hold it off! Take them and get out of here!"

## Chapter I: Inglis, Age 0

"But—Aunt Serena! That sword can't even scratch them!"

The lizard turned its baleful gaze on Serena. Even though she was no longer a knight, she could manage to parry its fierce assault. The problem was the unreliable blade she had at hand. Its thin construction couldn't bear many blows before bending into uselessness.

"Hurry! What are you waiting for?!" Serena barked orders at Rafael.

"Rani! Chris! Sorry, just hold on!" Hiding Inglis and Rafinha in the shade of a pillar, Rafael drew his sword and ran beside Serena. "I've got your back! If we can hold out a little longer, a knight with an Artifact will be here!"

An Artifact—that must be the sort of weapon modern knights wielded against magicite beasts.

"No! I told you—no! Get out of here!"

"I'm not going anywhere! If I can't save the people right here in front of me, how will I ever be able to save anyone?!"

His young voice, still high-pitched, nevertheless rang with passion. Inglis was growing to appreciate her cousin the more she saw of him. Fighting through danger and always rising to one's feet was what made someone a hero, not by being called one. It was proven through determination and effort.

"Ngh...ugh! Whoa!"

"Aaaaah!"

Yet as hard as the two struggled, eventually, they were slammed back into the wall.

"Aunt Serena! A-Are you okay?!"

"Ugh..."

The world was beginning to go dim around them. Soon, they'd be at the beast's mercy—and then, with them gone, there'd be no one to protect the unconscious Irina or the young Inglis and Rafinha.

*Guess it's my turn, then. I can't let my own mother be killed. And the boy's definitely proven his worth as well...*

Inglis had resolved to live her new life for herself. She had no interest in becoming a hero—but she certainly had no objection to helping out someone who did. It'd be a shame if he were to die here.

There wasn't much an infant could do, but… No harm in giving it a try. Even without moving a finger, she could smash the beast with raw, physical aether. It was a basic technique, one she'd known even in her past life. "Aether Strike," if she had to give it a name. She'd never tried it from her cradle, afraid of bringing the house down around herself, but here, with everything in shambles and every potential witness out cold, there was no reason not to.

"Daaa! Goo-goo, ga-ga-ga!"

Young as they were, Inglis's eyes had a clear sparkle. A pale blue flash of light welled up, transforming into a gigantic glowing bullet which smashed into the beast.

*Blammmmmm!*

The bullet then wrapped around the lizard-like creature, carrying its body straight through the wall. As it fell, it crumpled and burned away midair into a cloud of white ash in the wind.

*Not bad for a baby, I guess*, she thought. Her practice obviously had been time well spent.

Rafael, his back propped up against the wall, gasped in shock. "Chris?! Wh-What was—"

Inglis would have grit her teeth if she'd had full control over her jaw.

"We're saved…" He slumped to the floor, unconscious this time.

If he remembered it as a dream, or as a stress hallucination, so much the better. As she planned for the aftermath, Inglis felt a wave of exhaustion wash over her. Despite having such raw power, she was still an infant, after all.

Concerned shouts echoed up the stairwell from below. "Lady Irina! Rafael! Are you safe?!"

The reinforcements must have arrived. Perhaps she, too, would slip

## Chapter I: Inglis, Age 0

away into slumber. She'd wanted to witness everything, but her newborn body betrayed her.

When next she awoke, she was back in the safety of her own cradle, under her own roof. She could hear the voices of her mother and father, so they, at least, were safe.

For some time after, Rafael seemed to treat her with a bit of restrained awe, although he was still suspicious. With no adult willing to believe, however, that an infant had achieved such feats, and no sign of her power in the peaceful months following, even he began to believe that the stress, confusion, and pain had simply tricked his eyes.

Most importantly, though, Inglis now knew magicite beasts were something new in the world. From what she could overhear between her parents, the attacking creatures were among the smallest of their weakest form, and there were far fiercer foes yet to face. Her father had even mentioned some were powerful enough to lay a whole kingdom to waste.

A fascinating prospect. For now, then, to develop her own skills until she could battle one of those!

Thus, the infant Inglis went on.

# Chapter II: Inglis, Age 5

As peace returned, the days turned into months, the months into seasons. Soon, it was five years since King Inglis had been reborn with the same name. Her first few years had been spent with a body like any infant's—barely able to move and quickly exhausted when she did. At five years old now, she could finally run around as she wished.

She was still a child, though; she was weak. What more was there to do but train while she waited to grow?

"..."

She examined her appearance in the mirror in front of her. Her mysterious platinum blonde hair and vivid red eyes were impossible to miss. She was an absolutely adorable young girl, so cute that her face practically sparkled. One that would surely grow into a beautiful woman.

*I guess I'm cute now. I suppose I'd always wanted a granddaughter like this.*

The old King Inglis had never had children. Then again, the old King Inglis hadn't expected to be reborn as a girl either. Being a different gender had been a shock at first, but she figured harping on that detail after something as grand as reincarnation was in poor taste, and complaining about it five years later would be particularly ungrateful. She decided to take the situation as a reminder from the goddess to stay focused. Who knows what a strapping young master of the blade might be able to get up to? At least this way, she would have fewer distractions.

Besides, just seeing her own smile was heartwarming. Maybe she could get used to this... She watched a satisfied grin spread over her face.

"You really like mirrors, don't you, Chris?" one woman said.

"Oh, Irina, she loves them," another replied. "They're probably the only things that stop her from asking tons of questions."

Inglis promptly flushed red at the sudden attention focused on her.

These two beautiful women were sisters—Serena, who was Inglis's mother, and Irina, Inglis's aunt. Irina was the wife of Duke Bilford, and her younger sister had married Luke Eucus, the captain of the duke's knights. Born into this family, Inglis began her new life. Not only was she the daughter of the Eucus family, but that also meant she was the daughter of the knights' captain and a relative of the duke.

"I can think of worse things. She's so adorable—even she knows that," Irina said.

"Dearest aunt," Inglis spoke up, "I apologize for behaving in such an unseemly manner."

"And so polite too! Wherever did you learn those words?"

"I, uh... I don't really know. I don't do anything special."

"She's already reading, Irina!" Serena said, enthusiastic.

"That's amazing! She must be a genius!"

"That'd be quite the blessing."

"I don't think Rafinha's reading level is there yet, but it'd be nice if they got to play together once in a while."

Irina turned her head to look at her daughter, Rafinha, waving around a wooden sword. The girl had dark hair and eyes with a charming face. Like Inglis, she was five.

Inglis considered playtime with her five-year-old cousin akin to babysitting, but that actually wasn't so bad. It was like an opportunity to spend time with a granddaughter she'd never had.

"Hi-yaaah!" Rafinha yelled as she swung her practice sword, just to

## Chapter II: Inglis, Age 5

lose her balance in the follow-through a moment later. "...Oof!" She sat on the floor with tears in her eyes.

"Are you okay, Rani? Here, upsy-daisy!" Inglis said, using Rafinha's nickname. She pulled her cousin to her feet and patted her head.

"Waah... Chris..." Rafinha whimpered, using Inglis's nickname in return.

"You need to crouch your hips down a little and swing the sword like they do." Inglis pointed with the wooden sword to the men sparring nearby.

They were in the knights' training grounds inside the castle. The knights were in the midst of an energetic practice session, and the occasional yell or grunt added to the lively atmosphere. Sitting in a vacant corner, Inglis's mother and aunt had brought their children to watch and learn. If not for that reason, it would be odd to see two noblewomen in such an intensely sweaty atmosphere.

"Next, Rafael! I won't hold back, so show me what you've got!"

"Yes, sir!"

A boy in his early teens faced off against a middle-aged knight. Now thirteen years old, Rafael bore himself with an intense expression and a dignity that spoke to his well-bred upbringing. He'd already earned a reputation as a serious, steadfast hard worker.

"You can do it, Rafael!" Rafinha called out to her brother.

Rafael was the duke's son—that meant he was the next ruler of the knights training here. His determination to throw himself into the same training regimen he'd ask of them certainly didn't hurt morale. The boy had begun to acquire a glowing reputation across all of Ymir. In other words, he was the real reason Serena and Irina were present. The knights had planned a small tournament for later today, and they wanted to see how Rafael performed.

"Here I come! Raaah!" he shouted.

"You haven't got me yet!"

Rafael's wooden sword clattered against the older knight's. At thirteen, Rafael was still a growing boy and couldn't equal the knight in strength, but he made up for that with agility, a keen eye for spotting openings, and an understanding of his own advantages.

Rafael weaved around his opponent's blade, constantly probing with his own blows. As the knight raised his sword to push Rafael down, the older fighter switched to using more aggressive attempts to keep the boy at bay. He finally swung back for an overhand blow to crush Rafael's guard—but that was just what Rafael was waiting for. The boy swiftly darted forward and dealt a precise blow to the back of his foe's knee, forcing him to fall to the ground, before pointing the tip of the sword between the knight's eyes.

"Enough! Rafael wins!" announced Luke, Inglis's father and the captain of the knights.

"Mm! Excellent work, Rafael!" the knight cheered.

"My own arms are shaking now too," Rafael admitted. "I would've been in real trouble if that had gone on any longer."

Rafinha leaped in joy. "You're amazing, Rafael!"

"I'm impressed you were able to take on a real knight like that," Irina complimented her son.

"I mean, I didn't really do anything special," Rafael said.

Serena turned to her sister. "Looks like you've got your own little genius there, Irina."

"I suppose we both do," Irina replied.

It wasn't just the mothers who were impressed—Inglis was too. At this point already, only her own father was likely to best Rafael in a match. Well, Luke *and* herself. She was fortunate to have a father who could eventually serve as her sparring partner rather than having to go out and find one.

The next knight stepped forward to face the skilled boy. "Rafael! I'll be your next opponent!"

"All right! Thank you!"

However, this fight was no different. Rafael turned his opponent's own strength against him. Another, then another, threw their hat into the ring only to be handily overcome. Clearly, Rafael's first victory had been no fluke.

*He's definitely talented. As my vassal, he'd make an excellent guard captain or general... I'd like to see what we may accomplish together*, Inglis thought, pondering over Rafael's potential as she watched him spar.

A portly man strode into the training grounds, followed by his retinue. "Hail, Sir Luke! It's been too long!"

Inglis assumed from his presence that he was a part of a mercenary company or something similar, but that was incorrect. His group comprised the armed merchants of the Rambach Company. Men traveling between cities to peddle their wares in such a chaotic age could, of course, expect an occasional magicite beast as an unwanted customer. As a result, they'd taken up Artifacts to defend themselves, a choice that the kings and lords whose lands they traversed had accepted as entirely reasonable. Their relations with the Dukedom of Bilford were especially good, to the point where joint training exercises occurred. Today was one of those times.

Luke smiled as he greeted their portly leader. "Ah, welcome, Mr. Rambach. It's a pleasure to have the opportunity to share what we've learned."

"Indeed it is! I'm honored to be able to borrow your knights' sword arms for a few hours." Grinning, Rambach motioned toward a boy of around Rafael's age. "This is my son, Rahl. Rahl, say hello."

"It's a pleasure to meet you, Sir Luke. My name is Rahl." His face was slender, his eyes sharp, but he sounded a little nervous as he introduced himself.

"And you as well. Rahl, you seem to be about the same age as Rafael here. I'm sure you'd be able to learn much from each other." Luke called, "Rafael! Introduce yourself."

"Yes, sir!" Rafael replied with no hesitation, smiling and extending a hand to Rahl. "I'm Rafael Bilford. It's a pleasure. Looking forward to training with you."

"S-Same here!"

"Excellent, then! A match, after you've warmed up!"

At Luke's order, the knights and the merchants paired off and began to train. As far as Inglis could see, the knights were more skilled in general. Rambach's son, Rahl, was talented for his age, but he was still no match for a full-grown knight; he was just too young. Rafael was an exception to that rule, though. That boy was exceptional. In the end, the knights were likely to carry the day.

Inglis held that opinion firmly—until the bouts began.

At first, the knights held fast. Each bout was a one-on-one duel with the loser eliminated, and the merchants' numbers shrank quickly. When Rahl stepped into the ring, though, the tides of battle shifted. Knight after knight couldn't make a dent.

"Gah!" The current unlucky knight's wooden sword clattered to the ground as he was struck on the arm.

"Enough! Rahl wins!" Luke announced. That marked Rahl's tenth straight victory.

"Heh heh heh. It seems the knights have gone a bit soft," Rahl observed, his voice unmistakably brash following his string of victories. He was like a wolf in sheep's clothing. "I've heard you've been safe from the magicite beasts recently. Perhaps we've been fighting them all off ourselves. After all, there's no lack of customers on a battlefield."

Rambach's son had more pride than the knights were entirely pleased with, but their losses in actual combat made verbal sparring impossible. Pointing out their own exploits would only draw a sharper line under their losses, so all they could do was stew in humiliation.

The knights who'd lost to Rahl grumbled to one another.

"I'll be damned! What a rise to the occasion!"

"He didn't seem that tough when we were practicing earlier..."

"When I faced him, I couldn't fight like I usually do."

"Same here. Is he just really good at keeping his distance?"

Inglis mulled over the situation. *Are those just excuses, or...?*

Regardless of rank, each of the knights carried a Rune on their sword hand. They were true knights, not a gaggle of militia.

## Chapter II: Inglis, Age 5

*He must be using some kind of magic. Something that lets him overpower them,* she thought.

Why he'd choose to do so in training was its own question, but Inglis was more concerned with the knights' reactions. They didn't seem to notice at all. Having only the slightest background in magic would make Rahl's ability clear, especially since Rahl seemed to be no great mage.

Even a beginner mage could do such a thing: a simple cantrip to weight the limbs of all who saw. It wouldn't need to hold them down completely—just to make one's strikes leaden and steps dull. It seemed that the understanding of magic, or even recognition of it, was a lost art.

Had Runes and Artifacts obstructed its study? It was certainly an unpleasant wake-up call for Inglis, who'd established magic universities to encourage an understanding of mana throughout the realm. Before she'd done so, those with a gift for magic had been outed and shunned. There had even been witch hunts. She'd strived her utmost to stop such discrimination and integrate magic into her society peacefully. In her past life's twilight years, her efforts had appeared to have borne fruit. Ah, well.

"Impressive, Rahl...but I won't lose!" Even Rafael, bearer of one of the greatest Runes, didn't seem to notice Rahl's magic at all.

"It's an honor to spar with a future holy knight. Let's keep it clean!"

Those were big words for someone already working through the somatic gestures of his spell with a hand held behind his back. Inglis, the only person who noticed, could barely imagine anything more brazen. Though, admittedly, Rahl was an exceptional showman for his age.

Rafinha nervously tugged on Inglis's sleeve. "Chris, do you think Rafael's gonna win?"

"He'll be fine. I'm sure your cheers for him will make him fight even harder." There was nothing else Inglis could tell her.

"Okay. Do your beeest, brotherrr!"

Rafael answered her with a smile. "Yeah. I'll give it my all, Rani. Thanks." With that, he readied himself and faced Rahl. "I challenge you."

"And I accept!"

"Begin!"

At Luke's call, the fighters sprang forth.

"Here goes!"

Rafael aimed a forceful slash at Rahl. It was a single powerful blow, with all his might behind it. He wanted to fight fire with fire.

*No! No, that's not it!* Inglis could barely keep herself from shouting. At this rate, Rafael would be undone just like the others.

"Too slow!" Rahl blocked Rafael's downward strike easily. It might have overpowered the cunning boy if Rafael had used his full strength, but right now it was fruitless.

"Ugh..."

"Bwa ha ha! You're no hero yet! Not at all!"

Next came Rahl's counterattack.

Rafael shifted his stance in response to his opponent's own, but he was moving slower due to Rahl's magic. Not realizing what had occurred, Rafael expected his own usual swiftness, but his body was sluggish. He was only half-ready when the sideways sweep came at him, and at the moment their blades clashed, Rafael's hand slipped from the hilt. The wooden blade came flying directly toward Rafinha.

"Eeek!"

"Rani?!"

"Don't worry."

*Smack!*

Inglis caught it nimbly.

"Th-Thanks, Chris," Rafinha said, tears in her eyes.

"Good job, Inglis!" Inglis's mother exclaimed.

Her aunt had plenty of praise for her too. "Oh, thank goodness! Thank you, Chris!"

"Rani! Chris! Sorry! But thanks!" Rafael said.

Inglis rushed to return Rafael's sword. "Don't worry about it."

"Thanks again, Chris."

"Um. There's one more thing—"

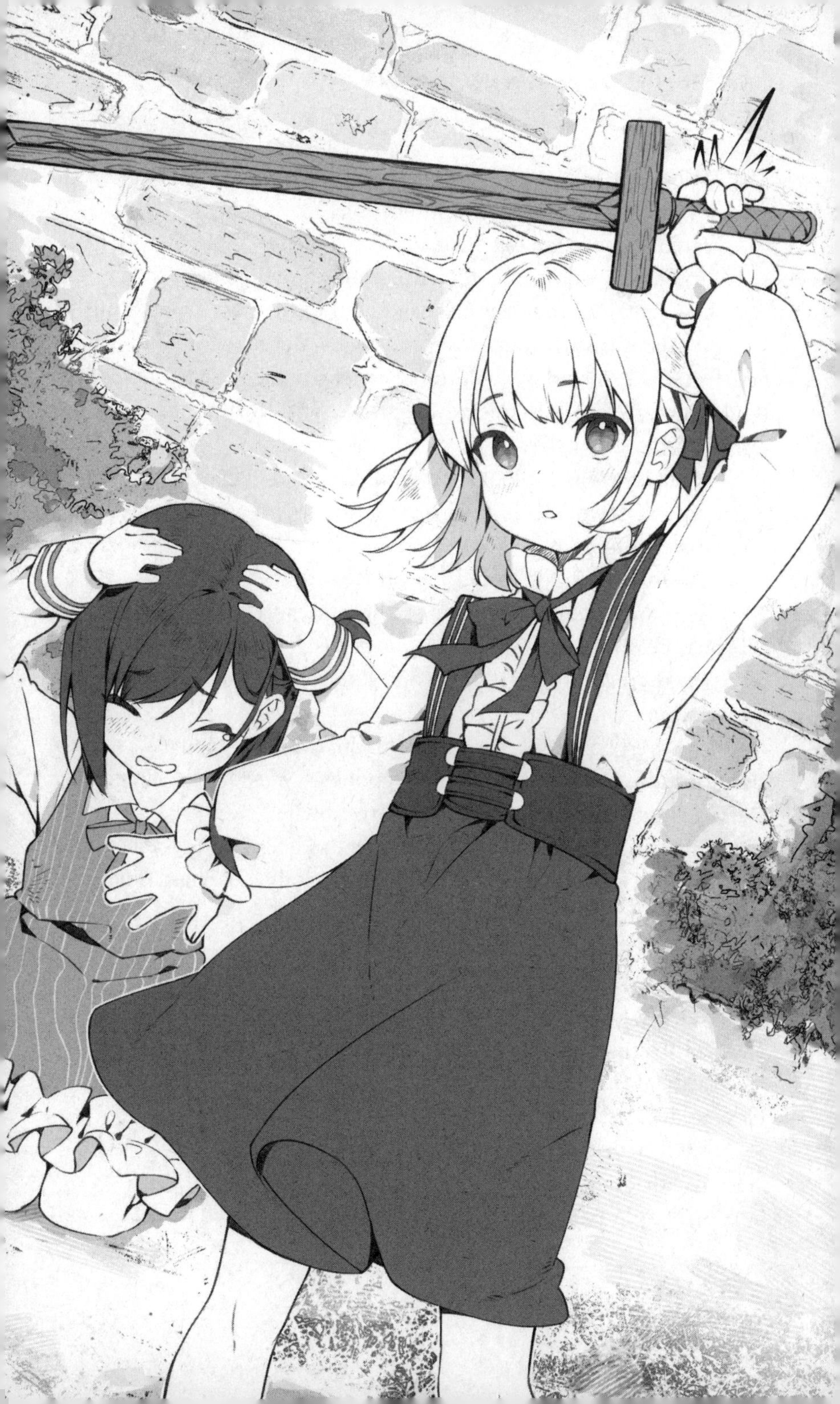

"What is it?"

"Try to look at him as little as possible."

"Huh? Why do you say that?"

"Something's not quite right. Everyone's moving slower than usual. Somehow Rahl's taking everyone head-on. I think there's something..."

No, she was sure. Rahl was using magic. But no one would believe her if she said so, and it would cause more trouble than it would help. Better, now, to lead him toward the answer and let him figure out the rest himself.

"Fight him without looking at him? I mean, I did notice something weighing me down... Got it, Chris. Thanks." With a nod, Rafael faced off against Rahl again.

"Pardon me, Rahl! Would you care for another round?"

"Very well. I guess that was just a half-measure. Maybe if I beat you till you're really hurt, you'll realize you've lost." Rahl had the cold glare of a snake regarding its prey, but Rafael studiously ignored the provocation.

"...Here I come!" Rafael rushed in, his gaze low to avoid catching sight of Rahl. He could watch his opponent's shadow on the ground instead. Rafael lined up a slash in its direction.

"Mmph...?!" Rahl swayed on his feet as he blocked. Rafael's new approach had nullified the effects of his magic. Rahl had a hard time holding his own in a battle of strength.

"I knew it...! Chris was right!" Rafael said.

"Grrr... Dammit!"

Rafael pushed Rahl farther and farther back until his foe was against a wall. This wasn't necessarily advantageous for Rafael, though.

"Graaah!" Rafael charged. Rahl barely managed to parry the first blow, and Rafael followed up with a slash from the side.

But it struck directly against the wall.

"Whoa?!"

So busy looking at the ground, Rafael had forgotten where the wall

## Chapter II: Inglis, Age 5

was. He slammed into it, staggered back, and that was Rahl's chance to strike.

"Ha ha ha! Got you!"

"Gah?!"

"Enough! Rahl wins!" Luke announced the result.

"Ahh!" Rafinha cried. "Wahhhh… Rafael lost…"

Inglis patted her on the head. "Don't worry. I'll settle the score."

It was bad enough that the knights had been taken down one by one in an unfair fight. She definitely couldn't let Rafinha cry about her brother's loss. After all, protecting Rafinha was Inglis's job.

Inglis picked up Rafael's wooden sword from where it had fallen and approached Rahl. "Not bad. How about one last match with me?" she challenged. A grin spread across her face.

"Gimme a break. What chance would a little girl have? I was hoping to take on Luke next." After frowning in confusion for a few moments, Rahl shrugged. "Why don't you go put on a dress and play with dolls instead? You're cute. I think they'd suit you better."

After a brief pause, Inglis fired back. "Would you rather I told everyone else what you were up to?" She took care not to mention exactly what he'd done. That would raise too many issues later. A leading question, on the other hand, could be explained away.

"B-Back off! You trying to accuse me of cheating…?!"

"Maybe. Maybe you should ask yourself if you're cheating. But how about it? Will you spar with me?"

"Whatever. Don't cry when you get hurt!"

"You neither."

With battle lines drawn, Inglis faced off against Rahl.

"Wait, Inglis! You're biting off more than you can chew!" Her father Luke, worried, tried to stop her as her mother Serena looked on worriedly.

"There's no need to worry, father. I am your daughter after all. It's my duty as well to protect the honor of our knights."

Most important to Inglis at that moment was the chance for a real fight. The next was to keep Rafinha from crying. Finally, she had to punish Rahl for his underhanded tricks. If he was already fighting dirty this young, he'd never grow into a proper warrior. He needed a better mindset.

"I mean, I'm proud of you for wanting to try, but…"

"If you don't let me, I'll tell mother you had to replace that vase."

"Do your best, Inglis!"

At least he was a reasonable man.

Thus, the match between Inglis and Rahl commenced.

"Begin!"

At first, Rahl merely watched her and stood still—as if he was casting a spell. Not that it would work on her. There was no way some amateur's magic could touch a divine knight. The aether wrapped around her would scatter it like a cloud of smoke.

It was no fun just relying on the aether, though. Sure, it'd be an easy win. An Aether Strike would put him in his place, but also in the ground. It was hard work to manipulate aether subtly enough for a sparring match.

What the moment called for was good old-fashioned swordplay.

And so she faced him down, though with her eyes closed. This would be a harder task than Rafael's attempts to follow his shadow, but what better way to test her skills? Especially her mind's eye—the ability to fight without vision. In her past life, she'd been adept at it when young, but the skill had atrophied after becoming king. This was a perfect chance to give it another try.

Thinking he could outwit her, Rahl circled behind her.

In silence, Inglis turned to face him directly.

"Tch!"

No matter what angle Rahl approached from, he found himself head-on with Inglis.

"Grrr…"

Her uncanny ability to follow his movements sapped his confidence.

## Chapter II: Inglis, Age 5

Slowly but surely, he began to feel unsure about his opponent. He abruptly pushed away those doubts and went on the attack. Surely, he told himself, it was a simple matter of physically overwhelming such a small child.

"Yahhh!"

He ducked around behind Inglis and slashed quickly before she could find him again. Yet Inglis was ready before he could bring his weapon down. Their wooden swords clattered together.

And Rahl's slid uselessly down hers to the side.

"?!"

Inglis had parried perfectly. A clash of blade on blade, a test of brawn, and she'd have been pushed back, but what she could rely on was skill to overcome force. With her sword held at an angle, even a little bit of strength at the right time was enough to direct his slashes away.

Then twice. Then a third time. Rahl's face went pale. *This isn't right!* he thought. *I should be hitting her, but my sword keeps slipping off-target!*

None of the knights, not even Rafael, had skillfully parried him like this. She was just a little girl—a little girl with her eyes closed. How was she so good?

"What the hell are you?!" he yelled, in the throes of panic now.

Even more shocked were Luke and Rafael. Rahl was no great swordsman without his magic and couldn't understand what was happening to him, but Inglis's father and cousin could see it clearly. Her technique was sharper than both Rahl's and theirs. How many years of practice would it take them to reach her level? Would they ever match her?

In a life-and-death fight, of course, things would be different. A shove, a tackle, anything to let them physically overpower her would be on the table. But in raw talent with the blade, neither could compare.

"Ha ha ha! I've got my own little prodigy!" Luke cheered.

"Wow, that's amazing, Chris!" Rafael said.

And as they gasped in awe, Rahl let out a high, desperate war cry.

"Graaah!"

He swung desperately, throwing his full weight into the blow in hopes it would land true. Inglis effortlessly parried, and Rahl's momentum sent him spinning down to the ground flat on his butt. This was exactly the chance she'd been waiting for.

*Smack!*

She brought her wooden sword down on his shoulder.
"Y-You got me!" Rahl admitted, his defeat certain.
"Thank you for the match," Inglis smiled as she curtsied. That had been a good fight. If she was grading herself, she'd passed. But there was room for improvement, still greater heights to attain. That was why she'd been reborn.

To no one's surprise, she received quite the jostling as Rafinha and her family, overjoyed, mobbed around her.

# Chapter III: Inglis, Age 6

Inglis was now six years old.

She gazed out the window of the living room before the family set out to depart. Rain filled the skies above the mountain pass not far away. It was not a natural rain. It glimmered with the colors of the rainbow.

This was a Prism Flow, said to give rise to magicite beasts. When bathed in it, beasts of nature transformed into magicite beasts and attacked humans. Humans seemed to be immune, but there was still plenty of work to be done getting livestock and the like under shelter. If every rose had its thorn, what must a thing of such beauty as a multi-color rain conceal? As beautiful a sight as it was, it was to be abhorred by the average human.

But to a decidedly non-average human like Inglis, it sent her heart racing in excitement. She needed a magicite beast that would put up a fight, one that she could test her limits against. Sparring with Rafael and her father was nice enough, but the best training was against a foe actually trying to kill you. Magicite beasts showed no mercy; they were the ideal opponent. *Rain more! Rain on the town! I need better practice!* she hoped.

Although Inglis was excited, her mother was in a melancholy

mood. "What an unlucky omen. And today was supposed to be your baptism..."

Today, she and Rani would receive their Runes. A Rune was necessary to control an Artifact, which was necessary to fight magicite beasts. For anyone other than Inglis, anyway.

A blade of normal steel couldn't harm them. Inglis had tried a few months before when a Prism Flow had fallen upon the town. She'd also confirmed that the aether-based techniques of a divine knight worked perfectly fine.

Inglis aside, Artifacts were needed to carve out an existence in lands where a Prism Flow fell, and thus Runes were vital. Runes were separated into lower, middle, upper, and special classes. The stronger it was, the stronger the Artifact it could control.

Rafael's special Rune was a one-in-ten-thousand occurrence. The strongest magicite beasts, fearsome enough to obliterate a kingdom, could only be taken on with Artifacts of that class. That had decided his purpose—he would prepare for an existential threat to the nation. Inglis could understand why her aunt was so insistent on his safety.

"A Rune..." Inglis mumbled to herself as she stared off into the distance. A divine knight didn't really need one, but...

In fact, as soon as someone got a special one like Rafael did, they immediately became the focus of the people's hopes. That much was easy to understand, just looking at Rafael. With that came the responsibility of fulfilling those hopes. That was the path Hero-King Inglis had already trod.

Inglis Eucus, on the other hand, wanted to live to master the blade. Every duty foisted upon her would be one more thing weighing her down. One more annoyance to deal with. That was what she was most afraid of. Anything but a special-class Rune!

"Now, Inglis..." Serena hugged her tightly.

"Mother? What's wrong?"

"This isn't the right thing to say just before your baptism, but...I really hope you don't get a special Rune. Those... I feel like those doom

## Chapter III: Inglis, Age 6

you to live and die for others. If that happened, you'd be taken away from me."

"What a coincidence, Mother. I was just thinking I'd like anything but that."

"Really? I know you're really interested in the knights, so I thought maybe you'd want that kind of power..."

"I mean, I am, but I don't want anything that's going to dictate how I live my life."

"Really? Then we agree! Anything but a special Rune! Remember to keep that in mind. I'm sure God will hear your prayers if you do."

"Understood. I promise."

"That's a good girl. Now, let's get going!"

Led by her mother, Inglis set off for the castle and her baptism.

◆ ◇ ◆

Luke greeted Inglis and Serena as they arrived at the castle. Beside him were Rafinha, who would also be baptized that day, and her family—that is, the ducal family.

That was how important baptism and receiving a Rune were, or so Rafael explained. He was fourteen now. Soon, he would leave Ymir for training at the knights' academy in the royal capital. He was grateful he was able to make it to Rafinha's and Inglis's baptisms before he left.

"Don't be nervous, Rani. I hope you get a good Rune. You too, Chris. I don't think I need to worry about you, though. You're sure to get at least an upper class! Maybe even a special class like me! I can't wait to see!"

The idea was significantly less exciting to Inglis than it was to him, but she still politely nodded. "Wouldn't that be wonderful."

"Ha ha ha. Always jumping to conclusions, aren't you, Rafael?" Luke gently chided.

Rafinha's father, Duke Bilford, chimed in. "He's right, Rafael. She may be good with a sword, but talent with a blade and qualification for a Rune are two different things, even if they go together a lot."

"Ah ha ha. So you and Captain Luke aren't worried either. I see you both smiling," Rafael said.

"Well, it would definitely come as a surprise," Luke admitted.

"He's right." The duke chuckled. "Though I'd certainly be proud if Ymir were to produce another great knight."

"My own Rune is middle class. It would be nice to see my daughter surpass me."

The baptism ceremony began with a cheerful, optimistic mood. An old man who must have been a priest took his place at the altar, mumbled a short invocation, and then invited Rafinha up beside him.

On the altar was a boxlike object made of some strange stone with a hole in the side, presumably leading to a hollow interior. This was, apparently, called the baptismal tabernacle, which granted Runes.

"Now, Rafinha, if you could place your hand inside."

"Y-Yes..." Nervously, Rafinha reached her hand into the tabernacle. As she did, it glowed and began to hum in resonance. "Oh, something's happening! Ah ha ha ha, it tickles! Don't worry, Chris! It's not scary!"

"Rafinha, you need to be quiet during your baptism," Aunt Irina scolded.

After a short time, the light faded, and the tabernacle fell silent.

"It is done. Rafinha, show us your hand."

"Yes..."

Rafinha pulled her right hand back from the baptismal tabernacle, and presented the back of her hand to the crowd. From it, the shape of a bow in pure white gleamed dimly.

The priestly old man raised his voice. "The Bow of Light! Congratulations, Rafinha! It's an upper-class Rune!"

"Huh?! Wow! Yay! Look, everyone!" Rafinha happily showed off her new Rune. The shape of the ward indicated what sort of Artifact it could control. The white gleam was proof of its class.

The ducal family members were all delighted.

"Rafinha! Congratulations! I'm so proud of you."

## Chapter III: Inglis, Age 6

"Rani! That's amazing! Great job! Remember to get plenty of archery practice!"

"Hahaha! Excellent, Rafinha! With you having an upper-class Rune, I can feel secure in Ymir's future!"

Luke nodded approvingly. "Rafael with a special-class one, and then Rafinha's being upper class! A pair like that will make wonderful leaders!"

"Yes, it's wonderful!" Serena did as well.

"Congrats, Rani. I know you'll make a great knight," Rafael said.

"Yeah! And this way I can still be together with you and Chris when we all grow up!" Rafinha had latched onto the idea that Rafael and Inglis were destined for greatness. She had said she wanted to be a knight to stay with her family.

"That's right," Inglis chimed in reassuringly. Well, Rafael was probably locked into that path, but Inglis had no attachment to the idea of knighthood. Fighting plenty of magicite beasts would be fine, but the more fame a knight acquired, the further they were pushed back from the front line to the sand table. In her past life, she'd gone along with that process, and somehow as she'd risen to the occasion, she'd also risen to the throne. That wasn't a regret, of course. She was proud that she'd managed to never let those around her down, but she also didn't want to go down that path again.

Thus becoming a knight would be fine, but if there was any indication she was going to rise in the ranks, she'd have to have plans to quit and become a mercenary or a merchant like Rambach. Her title didn't matter—what mattered was being in the thick of combat. That's what she wanted to do with her life.

"And next is Inglis. Step forward, please," the priest said.

"Yes, father."

It was her turn. Inglis stepped toward the baptismal tabernacle and, after composing herself, thrust her hand inside. As it had with Rafinha, the baptismal tabernacle glowed and began to hum in resonance.

It had begun to do its work. And touching it, she understood what that work was. *So this is made to crystallize the flow of mana into a Rune?* Most of the people of this new age lacked the sense that would let them manipulate mana and control magic, but that wasn't because mana was gone altogether. It was because the techniques for its use had been forgotten.

The Runes, which the baptismal tabernacle inscribed, were an automatic flow of mana. If one were to grip the hilt of an Artifact, mana would flow from the hilt into it.

Using mana was, in itself, casting magic. Because the people of this age lacked the knowledge of spells, it was plausible that the inscription of a Rune was a stopgap. *But if that's right...* Inglis began to ponder the implications. As she did, the light faded from the tabernacle.

"It is done. Inglis, show us your hand."

"Of course..." Inglis pulled her hand free and looked at its backside.

There was no Rune. It was the same delicate hand she was used to.

That made sense. A divine knight was half-human, half-god, clad in the divine will. Aether, not mana, swirled around a divine knight's body. There was no way a device designed to inscribe mere mana could affect them. That tabernacle was more likely to catch fire if it tried hard enough. There was no mana in a divine knight for it to even work with. At least it hadn't tried to inscribe a special Rune.

"Nothing happened." Inglis, relieved, held up her hand.

"Wha...?!"

The men of the family all sprang to their feet.

"Impossible! My Inglis, one of the Runeless? I can't believe it!" Luke gasped.

That was what those whose mana was too weak to be inscribed as a Rune were called. In Inglis's case the causes were the opposite, with the overflowing power of a divine knight simply shrugging off any attempt to inscribe a Rune. But even if the causes were different, the results were the same. Wasn't it ironic?

## Chapter III: Inglis, Age 6

"That's right! I can't believe Chris, of all people, would be Runeless! Something must have gone wrong!" Rafael chimed in.

"Is the baptismal tabernacle working properly? Check it!" the duke ordered.

Unwilling to accept what had just happened, they crowded around the old priest.

"Erm... It just worked on Rafinha, didn't it?" the priest said.

"It could have broken after that, could it not? Anyway, let her try it again," Duke Bilford ordered.

"Very well, then. Inglis, if you would."

She figured she may as well keep trying until her family came to terms with it.

She tried four or five more times. The fathers of the two girls, so puffed-up as the day began, were well and truly deflated. She felt a bit sorry for letting them down.

"I can't believe it," Luke said. "Without a Rune, she can never be a knight. Squire's as far as she'll get... She'll never take over as captain..."

"I'm sorry to disappoint you, father."

Luke shook his head fervently. "No! You didn't— I didn't mean that! Don't worry about it, Inglis!"

He must have been worried his concerns had hurt her. Being sure to correct himself was, she supposed, the sign of a good father. Though letting it slip to begin with was also the sign of a hasty man. *Better to not let out a peep to begin with*, she thought.

"There's plenty I can do even without a Rune," she said. "And I plan on achieving those things. If Rani will become a great knight, she'll need a squire by her side. I don't need an Artifact Sword to be her shield." Inglis smiled, an expression of true relief.

With no Rune, she'd never have to worry about rising above squire. This wasn't a setback; it was an advantage. No expectation to give orders meant no reason to leave the front line to issue them. And never having

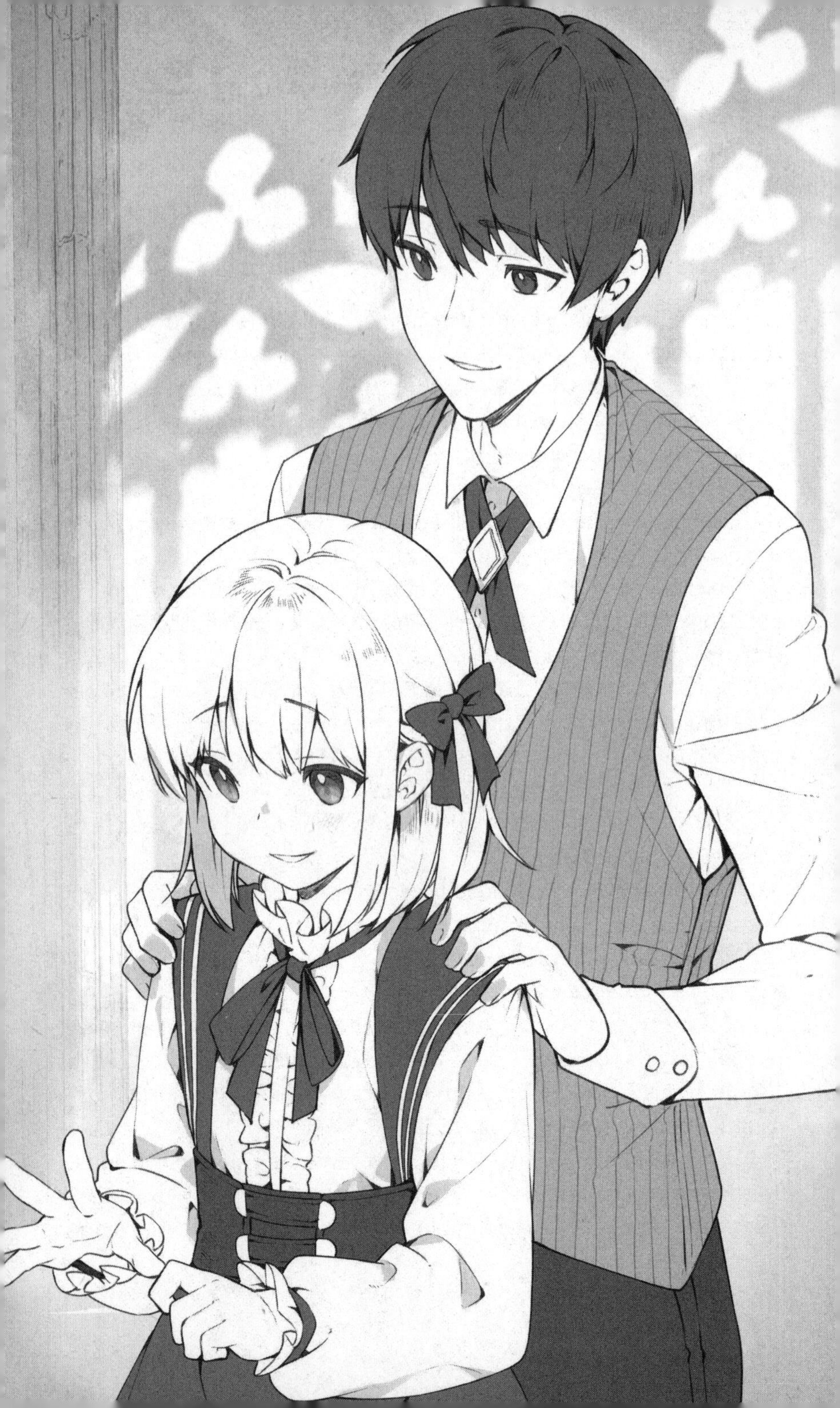

to leave the front line to climb the ranks was a great opportunity to focus on mastering the blade.

However, her family around her mistook her relief for a wholehearted effort to move along from bearing the weight of her disappointment.

Luke and Duke Bilford nodded gravely.

"I see. You're right…"

"Take good care of my Rafinha, Inglis."

Her mother and aunt could say nothing, only watch with tears in their eyes.

"Chris! Chris, you really are an amazing person!" A tear ran down Rafael's cheek as he hugged Inglis. He was deeply moved.

"Chris, I'm so happy. This means we can stay together forever." Only Rafinha could manage an encouraging smile.

And thus the day of Chris's baptism ended, even if it didn't end happily.

A few days later, Rafael left for the capital and the knights' academy.

# Chapter IV: Inglis, Age 12 (Part 1)

Six years had passed since the day of her baptism, making Inglis twelve years old and deep into a daily training regimen while conveniently helping Rafinha on the path to the knights' academy that her Rune, the Bow of Light, had set her on.

Luke, Inglis's father, had granted them both permission to participate in the knights' training sessions and hunts for magicite beasts, which were in many ways fulfilling experiences. Inglis thought it definitely wasn't a bad way to stay sharp, in any case.

Unfortunately, not one of the largest magicite beasts, the sort that could destroy an entire kingdom, had seen fit to appear. Inglis had heard only the strongest Artifacts—the ones wieldable by those with the highest, special class of Runes—were enough to take on those foes. Nonetheless, Inglis wanted to find out for herself.

Such beasts were said to have become rare in the environs of Ymir within the past two or three decades. Neighboring kingdoms were, however, less fortunate. Inglis hoped for a chance to be a part of an expeditionary force to those places.

When she'd mentioned that to Rafinha, her cousin had been aghast at the idea of fighting such dangerous prey, but Inglis wanted more. She wanted—more than anyone—to be stronger than everyone. Inglis Eucus would live by the blade!

That's what ran through her mind at least.

Before her was long platinum blonde hair that shimmered like the moon, dark red eyes that glimmered like rubies, and a smile that bloomed like a flower. This was her after twelve years. This was her reflection in the mirror.

She was tall for her age and looked a bit more mature for it. She figured she could pass for fourteen or fifteen. Spinning, she let the hem of her red dress twirl happily in the air.

*Hmm. My looks are coming along nicely too*, Inglis thought, considering her future. Along with all her talents, she'd be quite the beauty someday.

"Chris, are you done changing?"

"Yeah, I'm done, Rani."

"Oookay, I'm coming in, theeen!" Rafinha said, stepping into the dressing room. "Ohhh, wow! You look so grown-up! You're beautiful! Absolutely jaw-dropping! ♪"

Rafinha had grown into a lively girl with dark eyes and shoulder-length silky black hair. She seemed a bit innocent at first, but she was clever and always upbeat.

The third person in the room, a woman in her forties or fifties, let out a pleased sigh. "Really, you look great in that. If a dress could be delighted by who chose to wear it, I'm sure this one would be overjoyed." This woman was the master seamstress of the city as well as both a personal and professional acquaintance of the ducal household.

"Thank you," Inglis said. "I like this one."

The duo enjoyed visiting this seamstress's boutique from time to time and checking out various dresses. Mostly it was Inglis who tried them on; Rafinha enjoyed having someone to dress up, and Inglis had no objection to playing the model. It was an opportunity this reborn hero-king would get only as a woman, so why not enjoy it?

## Chapter IV: Inglis, Age 12 (Part 1)

In any case, it was a refreshing break from training. And as embarrassing as modeling dresses had been at first, she'd quickly gotten used to it. After all, she was in firm agreement that she looked good in just about anything. Imagining what aspects of herself she could choose to emphasize through different outfits was fun.

"Why don't you tie your hair up with this ribbon?" Rafinha asked. "I think you'd look really cute with it. ♪"

"Why not? Can you tie it for me?"

"Sure. I'll get that," the seamstress offered.

"Thank you, ma'am."

"It's fine. I'm a woman too. I deeply appreciate the beautiful things in life."

With her hair tied back, Inglis looked even more grown up. *Not bad at all*, she thought. *Beautiful, in fact.* Inglis smiled at the mirror.

"Wooow! That looks great too! It's perfect!"

"Isn't it? ♪ Now, how about these?" the seamstress said, holding some other outfits. "I thought you'd look wonderful in them, Inglis, so I set them aside."

"Go ahead, Chris! Try them on!"

"Ha ha ha. Sure."

The rest of the day passed, and evening fell. As Inglis and Rafinha headed home, they saw a gigantic shadow pass far above them in the sky.

It was a floating island—one big enough to hold Ymir and even its fortifications twice over. Atop this drifting island was a city.

"Wow, it's Highland! I haven't seen it in forever!" Rafinha closed her eyes and clasped her palms in its direction.

"What are you doing, Rani?"

"Making a wish! They say that if you wish on Highland, your wish will come true!"

*Like wishing on a shooting star*, Inglis guessed.

It was true—seeing Highland from Ymir was a rare opportunity. Inglis had only seen it once before. It was fascinating; it definitely hadn't existed in her previous life. She'd also heard that Artifacts and the baptismal tabernacle that inscribed Runes were crafted by Highland and endowed to the soil-bound kingdoms so that they could defend themselves.

"Wishing on Highland, huh... Sounds superstitious."

"Oh, stop being a stick in the mud! Just try it! Wish for something, Chris!"

"Fine..." She closed her eyes and made her one wish: *I hope I find an opponent with a bit of fight to it!*

"I hope Rafael is doing well," Rafinha said. Her brother had graduated from the knights' academy at the head of his class, but he remained in the capital to work. He was constantly busy and rarely had time to return to Ymir. It had been several years since they'd last met. "How about you, Chris? What did you wish for?"

"A challenging opponent...I suppose."

"Aha ha ha. Sometimes I think they messed up making you and put the soul of a warlord in the body of an angel."

"I'm not sure you're wrong."

It was a closer guess than Inglis wanted to admit. Rafinha definitely knew her well. They'd grown up these past twelve years practically as sisters, and Rafinha knew Inglis could fight magicite beasts without an Artifact.

"Anyway, I hope my wish comes true," Rafinha said, "but I'd rather pass on yours. Who knows what would happen if you got what you want?"

"That's not fair at all."

"Then wish for something cuter. Maybe 'I want to be swept off my feet' or something."

"Uh, nope, nope, nope...! No way!"

Just the thought sent chills down her spine. Dressing up? Looking good? Sure, but she was doing that for herself. Her body may have changed, but her tastes hadn't. Being drooled over by some guy was not on the menu in her case.

"Really, though," Rafinha continued, "I don't want you falling in love

## Chapter IV: Inglis, Age 12 (Part 1)

with anyone I don't know. It's Rafael or nothing. And no one but you for him!"

"I, uhh... I'm not quite sure—"

"Oh, whatever. Let's just go home."

They had both made wishes that night:

*I hope I find an opponent with a bit of fight to it!*

*I hope Rafael is doing well.*

And they would, by chance, both come true soon.

Several days later...

"A royal inspector?" Inglis asked.

"Yes, my father was talking about them," Rafinha replied. She had brought news of them during a break in the knights' practice. "A royal inspector comes every two or three years, but this is the first time they've brought someone from Highland with them."

"Hmm. I see."

"I've never met a Highlander before. I can't wait to see what they're like! Father said he'd like us to attend the reception, so we'll meet them there."

"Yeah. I guess we will."

Rafinha was excited, but was this really something to be pleased about? Highland was the source of the Artifacts by which the soil-bound lands defended themselves, but in return, Highland demanded vast quantities of crops and resources from the other lands.

It was a simple proposal: cooperate or die. Her country had so far kept its royalty and aristocracy, but surely Highland must be contemplating direct rule as well. Perhaps this was simply their first step in seizing control of the government.

This was all probably a bit beyond twelve-year-old Rafinha's grasp of geopolitics, admittedly. It was also far beyond the sphere of Inglis Eucus, who wanted only to spend her life as a squire on the front lines, no matter what habits she'd picked up in her past life. Still, she didn't want anything to happen to her family or to her home of Ymir. And if trouble was coming, she'd fight it with every ounce of her power.

Before long, the inspector's delegation arrived.

◆◇◆

A dressing room in Duke Bilford's quarters hummed with conversation.

"Amazing…! You look beautiful!"

"Really, like something out of a painting!"

"I can't believe she already looks this splendid…!"

The maidservants sighed in admiration.

"There we go," the seamstress said with a smile. "I've tied your hair up, Inglis. Really, though. What makes things shine is finding the proper place for them. And I think you're the perfect owner for this."

Tonight, a banquet would be held to welcome the inspector and their delegation. The seamstress had come to the castle to help Inglis prepare, bringing the red dress Inglis had tried on. Inglis's parents had bought it for her to wear at the banquet as a debutante.

"Thanks. It's a bit embarrassing, though." Inglis was drawing far more attention than she wanted. Showing off in front of her close friend Rafinha and the seamstress was fine, but being the center of strangers' attention tied her stomach into knots. In her past life as a king, she'd of course been the center of the attention of her subjects, but that was a different kind of attention.

"Inglis, you know every eye will be on you when you walk into that hall," the seamstress said. "Come on, give me a happy little spin like you normally do! Show me you can do it!"

"Um… Like this?" She twirled, sending her hemline hovering in the air for a moment and bouncing her tied-back hair. Her smile sent the maidservants swooning. "Uh, it's really embarrassing…"

"Come on. Don't slouch like that. You're prettier when you stand straight."

## Chapter IV: Inglis, Age 12 (Part 1)

Rafinha, wearing a yellow dress, smiled at Inglis. "Are you ready, Chriiis? Oh! I guess you are. Oooh. Looking as good as you always do! ♪" Her own dress and the flower in her hair suited her well. They weren't merely cute on her—they accentuated her naturally positive energy.

"You look cute, Rani. Really, you do."

"Really? I think I'm just a sideshow to you, Chris."

"No! You're adorable. I can't believe it. You were such a tiny little thing, and you've grown up so much." Inglis had perfectly clear memories of when they'd been babies. To her, it seemed like hardly any time had passed at all. Inglis may not have been a proud parent, but seeing how Rafinha had grown, she knew now how those parents must feel.

"Aha ha ha. You sound like my parents. Thanks, though. I'll take your word for it. I'm just a little nervous. We don't wear dresses that often."

"You two look wonderful! Everything's ready, then," the seamstress said, pushing Inglis forward lightly. "Go on!"

"All right, let's go, Chris!"

"Yeah."

Hand in hand, Rafinha and Inglis walked down to the reception banquet. It took place in the great hall on the first floor, facing the courtyard. As soon as they neared the entrance, a young knight with a gallant expression took them aside. Her name was Ada, and though she was still young, she was already the lieutenant captain of Ymir's knights. Luke had been sent to lead an expeditionary force, leaving her in charge of the guard.

"Why if it isn't Rafinha and Inglis! Your dresses are beautiful! You look adorable!" Ada was a close acquaintance and a constant companion on missions and training alike. As a young woman a bit older than they were, she kept an eye out for the girls.

"Thanks, Ada."

"Thank you."

"When you're ready, please make your way inside. His Grace is waiting. And don't forget to enjoy yourselves." Ada smiled, before frowning for a moment. "But it would behoove you to keep your guard up.

Anti-Highland guerrilla band activity is on the rise, even though I doubt they'd be active in Ymir. It would be very unfortunate if anything were to happen to their ambassador."

"You worry too much, Ada," Rafinha said. "Ymir's in the middle of nowhere. That may as well be happening in another world."

"Rani," Inglis cautioned, "with my father gone, worrying about that is Ada's responsibility. She's right. Let's help her keep an eye on things."

After all, Inglis would love the chance to test her own might.

"That makes sense. I guess I should take it as a compliment?" Rafinha's upper-class Bow of Light Rune outranked that of the knights. And while Inglis was Runeless, Ada knew quite well that she was a prodigy of the blade beyond comparison. That must have been why she'd even mentioned it.

"Of course," Ada confirmed. "Thank you."

Rafinha smiled. "Okay. Let's go inside, then?"

"Understood." Inglis nodded.

Inglis and Rafinha strode forward into the hall. As they did, all eyes gathered on them. Inglis felt their stares focused on her in particular—not that it mattered.

"Oooh! Everyone's looking at you, Chris!"

Rafinha puffed up with pride, but Inglis was significantly less pleased. The women watching were embarrassing, but she could endure them. She was beautiful to them in the same sense that a vista or a painting would be, but to the men... Even experiencing this kind of attention for the first time, Inglis felt it was completely different.

Inglis was twelve, but she looked more like fifteen, which was the age where men would start seeing her as a woman rather than as a girl. Her face, her hair, the graceful movement of her limbs, and especially the small cut-out above her chest—the men's gazes showered down like a storm on all of these features.

Her own eye had caught these things at the occasional banquet in her past life. Back then she had only thought of it as one person appreciating a beautiful woman, but now, on the other side of it, she sensed an immense pressure from that hail of stares, and it was not enjoyable at all.

How must those women she'd ogled have felt, then? It was a bit late to regret how she'd acted, but still, she regretted it all the same. That had been wrong.

"R-Rani…! Can I hug you?" Without thinking, Inglis stepped back into her friend's shadow.

"What's wrong, Chris? Everyone wants to see you. You don't need to hide."

"Th-That's why I *want* to hide! It's creepy!"

"But you look so grown up. Isn't it nice being so popular?"

"You have got to be kidding me."

*Maybe a woman with a more conventional background would enjoy this*, Inglis thought. But no matter what Inglis looked like, she still had her memories, and this was no more appealing to her than a room of men leering at her in her past life would have been. *How could I be anything but uncomfortable?*

"Umm… Anyway, why don't we go see the duke?" Inglis suggested with a tone of forced enthusiasm.

"O-Okay."

The sooner they'd made their introductions to the inspector's delegation, the sooner they could leave. Inglis half-dragged Rafinha in her search for Duke Bilford. Finally, she found him at the rear of the haul, engaged in light chat with a few others.

"Father!"

"Your Grace!"

The duke smiled as he noticed the girls approach. "Oh, Rafinha and Inglis! You look wonderful in those dresses. I couldn't ask for better centerpieces. I can hardly believe you've grown up so quickly." He turned to point them out to the group around him. "Let me introduce you. This is my daughter, Rafinha, and my niece, Inglis."

"I'm Rafinha. Pleased to meet you."

"Inglis. An honor to make your acquaintance."

The pair of girls gave prim and proper curtsies.

"Oh, you must be the girls Rafael mentioned. Glad to meet you!" A man in his late twenties, dressed in a knight's attire, flashed them a friendly smile.

"Ooh! You know Rafael?!" Rafinha exclaimed.

"Well, not closely," he answered.

"This is Sir Leon, another holy knight like Rafael," the duke said in introduction.

"A holy knight...!" Rafinha gasped.

They were knights who the king granted the strongest Artifacts. In other words, holy knights were the holders of special-class Runes. The back of Leon's hand had an unmistakable rainbow light.

"It's a shame I'm the one here tonight. I should have let Rafael come home, but he's so busy he couldn't spare a moment away." Leon sheepishly scratched his head as he laughed. Holy knight or no, his laid-back attitude was as evident in his wrinkled clothing and stubble as it was in his voice.

Duke Bilford continued the introductions. "This is the inspector, Lord Shiony."

A whiskered gentleman in his forties greeted them. "Ah, such beautiful young ladies. It's an honor to meet you."

"And this is the ambassador from Highland."

A young man sitting off to the side waved as he returned Duke Bilford's gaze. Unless Inglis was mistaken, this was a face she knew.

"R-Rahl...?!"

It was the son of Rambach, leader of the armed merchants, who had visited once before.

"Hey. Long time no see, Inglis." Rahl smirked.

He was just as she remembered. She hadn't been mistaken after all. But how in the world had he come here as a Highlander?

"So it is you, Rahl. A pleasure to meet again." Inglis curtsied politely.

"Isn't it strange, me becoming a Highlander?" Rahl was around twenty now, wearing a crest of feathers, and bore a Rune-like mark on his forehead.

And his eyes were a much more pronounced green than they had been.

"Yes, it is quite a surprise, honestly."

"I'd imagine. But there's no faking the stigmata. I'm absolutely the real thing."

"So you can become a Highlander without being born in Highland?"

"Sure can. Make yourself valuable enough, and citizenship is yours." Rahl proudly stroked the mark on his brow.

"Valuable enough, in what way?"

"One word: money. It took nearly every penny we'd earned. That, and some connections among the upper crust."

"I see."

To cut to the chase, he'd bribed his way in. That wasn't a very pleasant story.

"Now, it may have taken my fortune. But that's a small price to pay for such privilege, isn't it? When a Highlander claps, mere lords leap."

"I'm not particularly concerned with politics," Inglis said.

There was only one thing Inglis Eucus had her sights on: mastering the blade. It's not that she didn't understand politics or sociology, but she was reborn to *not* have to pay attention to them.

"Then what are you interested in? Travel, maybe? You grew up real pretty, maybe I could take you back to Highland and show you a good time."

That look on his face—she noticed him leering, and she wanted him to stop.

"Training. Becoming the best I can be."

"C'mon, quit pulling my leg. I can see you're Runeless. What good is training going to do? I know how prodigies work. By the time they're twenty, everyone else has caught up. But what you do have are your looks. The sooner you realize that and find yourself a man, the better."

"I'm afraid I'll have to pass for now."

"Really? I offer you advice from the kindness of my heart, and you just want to ignore it? Clock's ticking, sweetie-pie. I bet even this guy could take you down now."

Rahl turned his gaze to a tall man standing close to the wall nearby. He was tall—practically gigantic. He was easily two heads taller than average, and even more remarkable was an iron mask covering his entire face. At a banquet, no less.

"And he is...?" Inglis asked after a pause.

"My own personal bodyguard—a slave. It's good to be a Highlander. I told him to keep the mask on; you'd like his face even less without it." Rahl intoned dispassionately as the man stood motionless.

Inglis had no reply to that.

Nothing about Rahl seemed pleasant. Just talking with him made her think less of Highland.

"Oh, right!" Leon broke in from the side with an energy that cut the building tension. "There's someone else I'd like you to meet! She's quite memorable, so let's go see her!"

"What kind of person is she, Leon?" Rafinha asked curiously.

Meeting a holy knight like Leon was memorable enough. The same went for the Highlander Rahl. There were already plenty of memorable people they had seen today.

"Well, if you have a holy knight, what else do you have?"

"An Artifact? And if it's a special-class Artifact, that means..." Rafinha said, eyes gleaming. Inglis was sure hers were as well.

"A hieral menace! Girls love hieral menaces, right?"

Hieral menaces were entities that could transform into the powerful Artifacts only special-class Runes could power. It wasn't entirely clear whether they were more human or more Artifact, but they usually took the form of a young lady, taking on the shape of a weapon at will, and it was a holy knight who drew out the fearsome power of that weapon. Hieral menaces were seen as goddesses sent down from Highland in exchange for vast sacrifices, becoming the last hope for humanity on the surface. It was said that only a hieral menace and a holy knight together could stand against a magicite beast strong enough to obliterate a kingdom.

"Ooh! Ooh! I want to meet her! Where is she?!"

"No idea, so let's go find her! Follow me!" Leon beckoned to Inglis as he left the hall.

"Okaaay! Let's go, Chris!"

"Yeah, coming."

Leon was probably trying to pivot them away from their conversation with Rahl, which was nice of him. Nothing productive was going to come of that chat. She was grateful for his thoughtfulness.

"Ugh, just listening to that guy really ticks me off. I'm glad I had you two to give me an excuse to get out of there. Sorry for using you like that." Leon grinned. Maybe he'd done it for himself after all.

"I agree, that wasn't fun at all. Right, Chris?" Rafinha seemed just as displeased as Leon.

"Yeah, a bit."

Inglis had been right about Rahl. He really hadn't turned out well.

"I wonder if all Highlanders are like that. If they are, I can't see myself liking them that much," she said.

"I meet a lot of 'em, and yeah, that's pretty much the whole story. Even the born ones." Leon shrugged. "They probably think we're some kind of subhumans crawling in the mud. I mean, it's true, without them deigning to provide Artifacts we'd never be able to protect our homes. But it's probably just a game to them, seeing how much bowing and scraping they can get for an Artifact."

Leon was probably right about the relationship between Highlanders and those below. He definitely had more experience with them than Inglis could get in a backwater place like Ymir.

"But they're the ones holding our lifeline," he continued. "So no matter what we really think, let's put on a smile in front of them. You two are cute, and you'll be fine young ladies soon. It may be a little bit humiliating, but if a hand happens to fall on your chest or your rear, it's probably better to just put up with it. I've gotta do plenty of ass-kissing too, right? If he wants his boots licked, it's just what's gotta be done."

Grinning while he said that? Maybe he was a pushover. Inglis wanted to move the conversation on. "Heh. Looks like you know how to keep yourself alive."

Rafinha, though, had other ideas. "I wish a holy knight wouldn't say things like that."

"Huh?"

"You're a holy knight! You're supposed to be our shining star of hope! Who do the weak have left to rely on if that's what you have to say?"

"That stings," Leon said. "But sorry. I took the joke too far."

"Ah... S-Sorry! I didn't mean to talk back to you like—"

"It's fine. I can tell you're definitely Rafael's sister with that kind of determination. You've really got your head screwed on—ah, there she is! There's our hieral menace! Right this way!"

Inglis and Rafinha followed Leon into the courtyard to the shade under a tree where a woman stood, sipping a glass of wine. She looked to be in her late teens and had glittering blonde hair and deep blue eyes that Inglis thought anyone could sink into. This was the first time Inglis had seen another girl as beautiful as herself or Rafinha. Yet even at a diplomatic reception, she was in a knight's armor. At her waist hung a pair of swords. Setting herself apart from the crowd gave her the proud aloofness of a cat, yet there also seemed to be a loneliness lurking beneath.

Nonetheless, Leon approached the slender young lady as casually as anyone else. "Hey, Eris! Why be gloomy out here when you could be having fun inside? There's plenty of good food."

The girl—Eris—sighed. There was that catlike demeanor again, like he'd annoyed her. Most surprising to Inglis, though, was that she seemed exactly like any other standoffish young beauty. So this was a hieral menace? A transformed Artifact? If Inglis wasn't seeing it with her own eyes, she wouldn't have believed it.

"Because I'd rather be out here. Don't worry about me."

"C'mon. I brought guests. I'd like you to meet these two."

"Huh? Why?"

"This is Rafael's sister, Rafinha, and his cousin, Inglis!"

Eris's eyes widened in anger. "You fool! Stop this!" she suddenly shouted. She didn't stop at words. She struck Leon, sending him staggering to the side.

"Owww! Why'd you hit me? They wanted to meet you!"

The sudden violence shocked both Inglis and Rafinha.

"Ah… Is it something we did?" Rafinha asked.

Eris turned away. "I-I'm sorry…!" With that, she turned and marched away.

Rafinha, still shocked, turned to Leon. "Er… Did we do something wrong?"

"Sh-Should we apologize…?" pondered Inglis.

"Nah, it's fine. Nothing you did. I just picked the wrong time to bother her. Sorry to scare you like that. Why don't we go back in, have dinner, and I can tell you all about how Rafael's doing? You're anxious about him, right?"

"I'd love to hear about Rafael, but…I'm curious about Eris too. Aren't you, Inglis?"

"I am, yeah."

"I don't think she's gonna be in any more of a mood for conversation if we push her. It's fine. I'll smooth things over and definitely get you together before we leave. But let's focus on Rafael for now."

"I guess. Is he doing well?" Rafinha really was anxious about her brother.

"Yeah, he's fine. He's a real sharp guy, so he's really making a name for himself in the capital. Lemme tell you all about it."

Rafinha paused for a moment before saying, "Sure! ♪"

In the end, Rafinha was back to her happy smile. Inglis's eyes narrowed in a grin. Rafinha's wish had been that Rafael was doing well, and hearing of his exploits was sure to reassure her that he was. Maybe her wish really had been granted.

"Eeek!"

Screams from the great hall suddenly cut through the air.

"What...?! What's going on?" Rafinha cried.

"Let's check it out, Rani!"

Anything causing that much of an uproar had to be a serious matter. Inglis took the lead as they returned. All eyes were fixed on the rear of the room. As they stepped further in, a stomach-turning odor rose to her nostrils.

Burnt flesh. It was a smell she remembered from the battlefield. The scene she began to take in reminded her of the past. At the far end of the hall, a burnt form tumbled to the floor near Duke Bilford. The body belonged to the royal inspector, Lord Shiony, whom she'd just met.

Scarred. Motionless. Dead as a doornail.

Nearby were Duke Bilford himself; Ada, the lieutenant-captain of the knights; Rahl the Highlander; and his guard. Duke Bilford and Ada gasped as a brazen smile rose to Rahl's face. Who knew what expression the giant wore beneath his mask?

"Wh-What in the world just happened?!" Even Leon's voice wavered.

"Hmph... I disposed of an eyesore, that's all. He wasn't showing a Highlander the proper respect." Rahl laughed coolly as Duke Bilford and Ada stared.

"Ada! What happened?!" Inglis cried.

It was only Inglis's hand on her shoulder that snapped Ada back to reality. "Inglis! It... It's my fault! It's my fault Lord Shiony—"

"What's going on? Calm down and just tell me what happened."

"R-Rahl...ordered me to be his companion for the night..."

"What?!"

What a creep. It was truly depressing to know he'd grown up so rotten. There were some things Inglis just couldn't understand even after having lived a life as a man. If a subordinate had done this when she was king, the punishment would have been swift and severe.

"When I hesitated, Lord Shiony came to my defense. I'd noticed

## Chapter IV: Inglis, Age 12 (Part 1)

sparks flying between them during the inspection… But when Lord Shiony got angry, Rahl brought forth a flame and—!"

What Ada was describing didn't sound like an Artifact. So it must have been something she couldn't sense—presumably, magic. Rahl had used magic as a child too. It had probably been a gift from his Highlander connections.

"And he did that to Lord Shiony?"

"Y-Yes…! I'm so sorry! If I hadn't—"

"Ada. You don't need to say any more. It wasn't your fault. Right, Rani?"

"Exactly! Chris is right, Ada!"

"O-Oh, what a mess…" Leon said. "It's partly my fault, I'd noticed them clashing because Lord Shiony was such a serious man, but…"

*An excellent choice as inspector, then*, Inglis thought.

"But what does it matter?" Rahl said nonchalantly. "I can just say he fell ill on the journey and died. A Highlander's word is as good as gold."

"I guess we don't have a choice," Leon said after a pause. He slumped his shoulders. "His Majesty couldn't argue with a Highlander, even if he wanted to."

"Meaning, of course, Duke Bilford, it's entirely up to me whether Lord Shiony passed away after a swift illness…or whether he was assassinated in a vile plot. I'm sure you understand what I'm trying to say."

"You'd dare…!"

"So order that knight to do exactly as I say. I want to see you sell out your own loyal soldier to save yourself."

"Is… Is this behavior all a Highlander amounts to?!" Duke Bilford yelled.

"Father…!"

In other words, Rahl wanted Duke Bilford to humiliate himself in front of his own daughter. Inglis could hardly imagine anything more cruel. But if it had come to this…

"Wait! I…!" Ada started to say.

The young woman was trying to sacrifice herself. That was to be expected. But Inglis pushed her aside and stepped forward.

"Ada, no," Inglis said. "Rahl, you're twisted. Is this what you call fun?"

"Absolutely! It was worth the shirt off my back and more! I get to trample all over the stuck-up useless worms who give themselves fancy titles, and their knight sidekicks too! It's the most fun I've ever had! Ha ha ha ha!"

"You are despicable."

"Hmph. Don't get full of yourself just because you beat me once. There's nothing you can do. Unless you'd rather take that knight's place for the evening?"

"A fascinating offer. Maybe I'll take you up on that."

Rafinha gasped in shock. "Wait, no, Chris! What are you thinking?!"

"She's right, Inglis!" Ada protested. "How could I ever apologize to Captain Luke?"

"Rahl has a grudge with me," Inglis said after a pause. "And he was after me earlier. So it should have been me to begin with." Inglis quietly reassured the two before turning back to Rahl. "Promise me. Promise you won't lay a finger on Rani or Ada."

"Good enough. You may be young, but you're the best catch here." Rahl smirked as his spirits soared.

Inglis, the bane of his childhood ego, had grown up into quite the flower, and now she was his to pluck. To subjugate her, to conquer her. Revenge, revenge! The respect he'd been denied! To him, this was a chance to salve his wounded pride!

"Then come to me alone—tonight. You won't want to find out what happens if you come tomorrow."

"Understood. I will." Inglis nodded, expressionless.

"I'll be seeing you later, then."

With that, Rahl left the hall.

# Chapter V: Inglis, Age 12 (Part 2)

Once night had fallen and she had finished her preparations, Inglis marched forth from the castle. Rahl was staying at the ducal villa on a nearby hill, and she made her way there alone through the deserted nighttime streets, clad not in a dress but in the standard-issue squire's brigandine she wore while on patrol with the knights.

The outfit wasn't her own, though; it was a loaner set from the castle armory. She didn't want her mother to worry. Rahl may have been attempting to cut off her avenues of escape by insisting she see him tonight, but the timing fit her own plans quite well. She'd be able to finish things before her mother ever found out.

Rafinha had pleaded quite loudly with Inglis not to go alone, but the duke's own teary-eyed intervention to keep his daughter from putting herself in danger had given Inglis the opportunity to slip away.

"Well, it's do-or-die, I guess," she muttered to herself.

Inglis was, of course, not planning on giving Rahl what he wanted, and she was reasonably sure he wasn't expecting it either. Even if he was cocky enough to think he'd cowed her into submission—thanks to his power as a Highlander—he would surely have a backup plan. She might also have to deal with the man in the iron mask and the flame magic that Rahl had used to kill Lord Shiony—or something very much like magic.

Even alone, he would likely be stronger than he'd been when they had previously clashed. Hopefully strong enough to be satisfying, this time.

"Hmm?"

Duke Bilford's villa, where Rahl presumably lay in wait, came into sight. At its gates stood the masked man. Inglis approached him and bowed politely.

"Good evening," she said. "Inglis Eucus. I believe I have an invitation."

Silently, the man pushed open the gates, which swung open with a metallic creak, before turning back around and nodding to Inglis that she should follow.

She meekly followed. The villa courtyard wasn't particularly large, but it did include a promenade lined with carefully-pruned trees leading up to the portico. They walked in the darkness with the sound of their footsteps as their only companions. When they reached the halfway mark of the promenade, the man suddenly stopped.

Inglis stared quizzically.

"I'm sorry," he whispered haltingly.

*As terrifying as his appearance is, he seems to be a more decent man than his master,* Inglis thought. *How painful it must be for him to have to silently watch Rahl's behavior.*

Inglis smiled. "I appreciate your concern, but I'm sure I'll be fine."

He said nothing more and walked on.

As they reached the end of the promenade, a silver flash from the trees pierced the darkness in an arc with unnatural speed and force toward the masked man.

He flinched. Twin beams of cold light pierced his neck, and he crumpled to the floor, struck down in the blink of an eye.

"So fast!" Inglis gasped.

It was an impressive attack, and as unfortunate as it was for the masked man, she was more interested in the blade that had delivered the blow than she was concerned for him. The sword was undeniably lethal, yet beautiful in its own way. It was enough to make her shiver in

## Chapter V: Inglis, Age 12 (Part 2)

excitement—not in fear. Its wielder was a blonde, sapphire-eyed young woman who approached Inglis with haste but no malice.

"Eris?" Inglis was sure this was the hieral menace Leon had attempted to introduce her to. Why was she here?

"Yes. You don't need to be here. Get out while you can," Eris warned.

"Did you come to save me?"

"Kind of. I heard what happened from Leon. And you're Rafael's cousin, right? I couldn't let anything happen to you."

Eris's new, friendlier disposition was quite the surprise to Inglis, but she remained steadfast. "Thanks. I can't turn back now, though. There's no telling what Rahl would do if I don't show."

She expected full responsibility for the inspector's assassination would fall upon the Citadel of Ymir—specifically Duke Bilford—at the very least. Rahl needed to be stopped now.

"Are you planning on just throwing yourself at him? Have more self-respect than that!" Eris demanded. "I'll handle him myself."

"Handle him how? Do you plan to assassinate Rahl? That's too dangerous. Think of what will happen to Ymir."

After a pause, Eris stubbornly refuted, "It's none of your concern. Just go home!"

"I refuse."

"You're an arrogant little brat, aren't you? One more step forward, and I'll attack. If you don't want to end up like him," she said, gesturing to the masked man on the floor, "then get out of here!"

Despite the harshness in her voice and her brandished sword, Eris's thoughts were focused on the apology she couldn't say aloud. *Sorry. I don't have a choice.*

It was a shameful thing for a hieral menace to intimidate a girl, but it was for Inglis's own sake. Eris didn't want to scare her, but Inglis was obviously determined, and Eris didn't have any time to explain.

"Ha ha ha ha." Inglis didn't turn and flee—just the opposite. She laughed with a mix of glee and self-confidence, her eyes gleaming with an unfathomable fighting spirit entirely different from the nervous young girl she'd appeared to be. "So we'll get to fight if I keep going? I'd love to."

Inglis stepped confidently toward Eris, her face beaming in innocent enthusiasm.

"Well then, at the ready," the battle-hungry girl said.

Inglis wanted to see just what a hieral menace was made of anyway. They were pretty impressive, if that earlier swordplay was any indication. Plus, this was a perfect chance to test her own skills.

Rahl could be dealt with afterward. She was sure he was itching to get his hands on her, so why not let him stew? She couldn't let this opportunity slip away. If she asked Eris to fight her in any other situation, she'd probably refuse or hold back. This was Inglis's chance to see how the hieral menace fought for real.

Eris sputtered, "You idiot! What are you thinking?!"

While her blade was at the ready, she had always intended to simply scare off Inglis. Yet here the girl was, practically overjoyed at the idea of a fight. She had no Rune. What was she thinking?

"Wasn't this your idea to begin with?" Inglis retorted.

"Yeah, but... Ugh!" Eris shook her head.

Eris reminded herself all she needed to do was get Inglis home. The girl must have lost her mind. Why else would she have offered herself up to scum like that? Eris would scare her away.

The hieral menace slammed one foot against the ground to startle Inglis before springing forward more quickly than she thought Inglis could react. She planned to feint, giving Inglis a near-miss blow just short of striking her face. Surely it would send the girl fleeing. However, as Eris's right hand descended to deliver the slash, it suddenly stopped in place.

Eris's jaw dropped. Inglis had not only caught her arm—she had completely overextended it.

## Chapter V: Inglis, Age 12 (Part 2)

\* \* \*

Grasping Eris's arm, Inglis flipped her opponent onto her own back before throwing her toward the wall of the villa. "Haaah!"

But Eris was quick to react. She found her balance again, planting a foot on the wall to rebound toward Inglis.

"Not bad!" Inglis dodged a follow-up slash by a hair's breadth while Eris landed in a cloud of dust and leaped to the attack again.

Eris's speed and her ability to roll with a blow—she was far greater than the knights of Ymir. But Inglis still felt her opponent was holding back. She would draw out a real fight, then!

"Why do you look so happy?!" Eris yelled, spinning her swords in a dance of death as she advanced on Inglis in a flash.

"I love a good fight!" Inglis unsheathed her own sword, blocking and parrying Eris's attacks.

"You're a real handful, you know that?!"

The clashing of their swords filled the night air with sparks and echoing clangs, and the panic of battle began to cast its pallor over Eris.

Inglis wasn't moving her legs at all. She was able to fend off anything Eris threw at her without repositioning. Eris had two swords. Inglis had only one. It shouldn't have been difficult! Especially not for a hieral menace; Eris was a match for any holy knight, and she was dual-wielding swords, her specialty.

Eris thought Inglis was one of the best swordfighters alive. She was parrying effortlessly. Her skill, her reactions, her predictions—something wasn't right.

Eris didn't understand. No matter how skilled of a fencer Inglis was, Eris should have had the upper hand physically. She was far stronger than a normal human. A knight with a Rune and an Artifact would be able to keep up, sure, but she was a hieral menace—an Artifact with a soul! This should have been impossible, yet Inglis was doing it.

Something was wrong, and Eris didn't know what. It wasn't magic like a Highlander would use.

"Show me what you've really got!" Inglis barked.

"I am!" Eris shot back. She assumed Inglis was referring to her ability with a blade.

But then, Eris found her chance.

*Claaang!*

Inglis's sword shattered into uselessness. It was purely a matter of weapon quality—Eris was armed with weapons specially made for a hieral menace, while Inglis had only the blade a rural knight would use for minor threats. The difference between the weapons was obvious.

Inglis gasped.

"Haaaah!" Seizing on the chance so intently that she forgot to hold back, Eris carved at Inglis one more time. Even a prodigy couldn't dodge that strike. The edge of the blade sliced down Inglis's arm.

Inglis, flinching, had thought she'd be able to twist away, but Eris had judged the range perfectly.

*Now that's how a hieral menace should fight,* Inglis thought. *I messed up and paid the price.*

That's what she'd wanted—a good, challenging fight. It was a minor wound, nothing to worry about. Plus, being without a sword meant things would start to be interesting.

"Oh..." Eris, though, suddenly pulled back, concern in her eyes. "A-Are you okay?"

Her attack had been a reflexive strike with all her might. She was glad she hadn't hit Inglis harder...but it still wasn't enough to scare her off.

*An opening like that should have left her dead, but... She may be young, but she's incredible,* Eris thought.

This concern elicited only disappointment from Inglis. "Don't ask me that, Eris. It makes it sound like you think I'm not a worthy opponent."

"It's not that, just—"

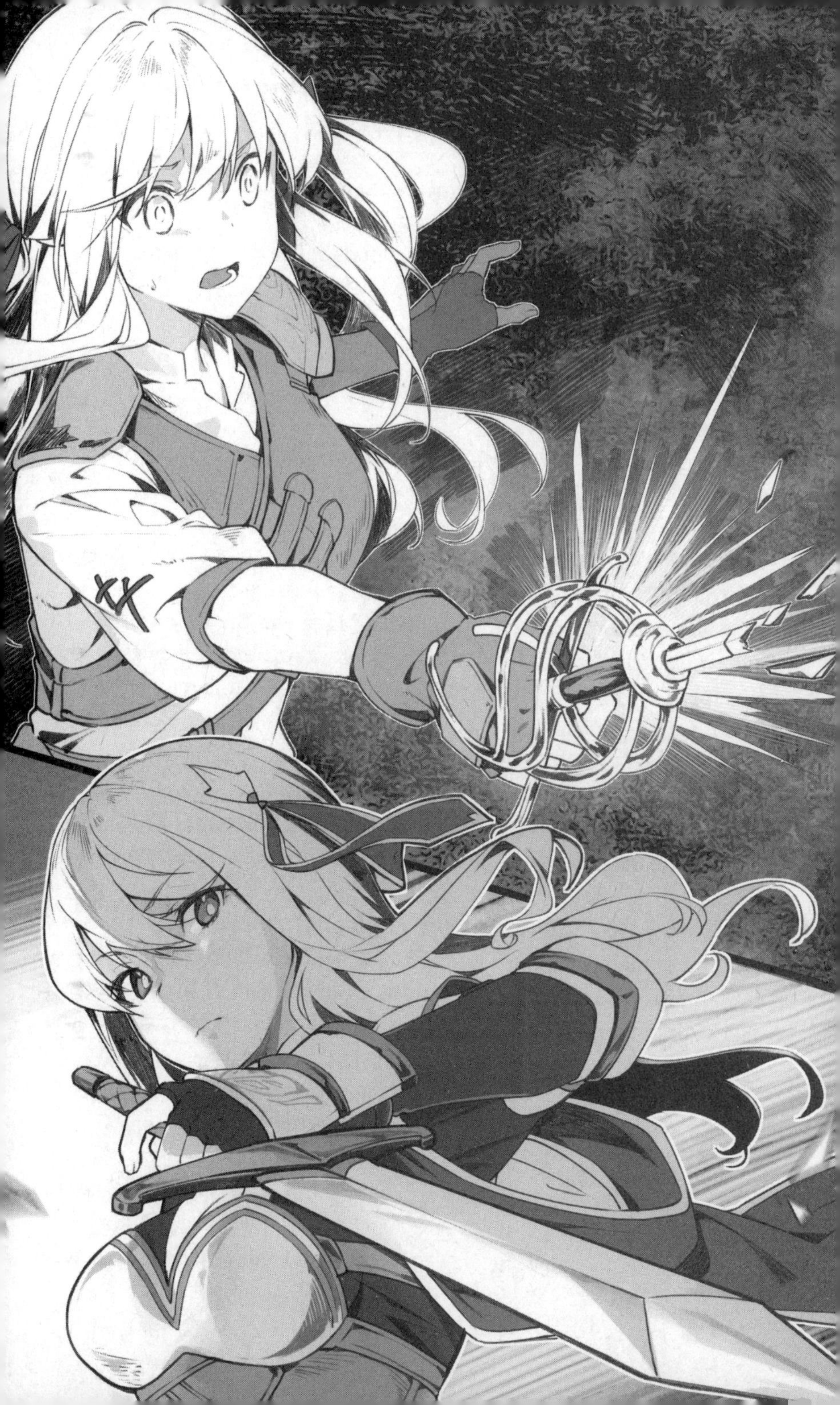

"Eris, tell me: can a hieral menace sense mana?"

"H-How do you know about that?!"

People from the surface weren't supposed to even understand mana as a concept. Inglis didn't even have a Rune!

*So how could she...?*

"Don't worry about that. Just answer me."

"Yes, we can. Somewhat, at least."

"Oh, good."

Eris couldn't understand where Inglis's carefree grin was coming from.

"If that's the case..." Inglis took a deep breath and focused. This was her chance to show off what she had been practicing.

She would convert aether to mana. Mana was the source of magic, and the source of power for Artifacts, but it was extremely inefficient. For example, only about a fifth of the mana focused into a flame spell would actually spring forth as fire. The remainder dispersed into nothingness. Aether lacked that flaw. A strike with aether would deliver the full force behind it, if not amplify that force. So strictly speaking, converting aether to mana was a waste. In this situation, though, against a foe like Eris, who could sense mana but not aether, that conversion had its own advantages.

"Ah! Wh-What?!" Eris gasped involuntarily as she sensed a massive amount of mana swirl around Inglis. "What the hell are you?!"

Eris had never detected anything from her before! Inglis had been just a normal girl without so much as a hint of special powers. That's why she'd wanted to stop her from going inside.

The girl in front of her now was completely different.

*She has enough mana to swallow me whole!*

Inglis grinned as she spoke. "Understand now? You don't have to hold back."

Eris had to know she was a worthy opponent. The hieral menace

## Chapter V: Inglis, Age 12 (Part 2)

would fight her on the same level after having sensed Inglis's converted mana.

Aether was the source of all things. Everything was made up of different concentrations of aether, which was why Inglis could use it to generate mana. Although it was inefficient, the process had its use here. Eris had been pulling her punches because she thought Inglis didn't have any power. Inglis had to make her understand.

And even though practicing the precise command of aether so Inglis could make her parents happy by being able to have a Rune hadn't panned out—since she lacked the mana for a Rune to appear—that training had taught her control.

"W-Well, then. I guess you don't need my help." Eris sheathed her swords. "I won't stop you. Go ahead."

"Huh? Wait! Wait, no! Please, no!"

"Wh-What? I thought you were just a little girl, but you've obviously got the mana to handle things. So there's no need to stop you."

"Gaaah! Anything but that! Ugh, what have I done...?" Inglis slumped in regret. She had finally found a foe of merit but had to prove her own worthiness. Yet all that had done was prompt her opponent to withdraw from the fight.

*I messed up. How frustrating. And right when it was getting fun!*

"N-No! I'm just a weak little girl! Come on, stop me! Please!"

"I've seen enough to know you can handle yourself. Better not to keep the Highlander waiting, right?" Eris spun on her heel and made her way back toward the gate, her business done.

"Ugh..." Inglis knit her fingers together in regret as she watched Eris leave. "I never should have done that! I'll never forgive myself!"

Then something suddenly pummeled Eris.

◆◇◆

A clap of thunder sounded and surges of electricity swirled as a beast, formed of crackling lightning, smashed into Eris from the side.

"Ngh?!"

It was like a thunderbolt had slammed into her. The beast's momentum carried her into the wall of the villa before it darted away.

"Ahhhh!" Eris's shriek could be heard over the rolling thunder as the beast's lightning smashed the wall around her.

"Eris?!" Inglis yelled.

The attack had caught Eris completely by surprise. "Ugh...," she grunted as she struggled to her feet.

"Are you okay?!"

"Yeah, somehow."

She wasn't critically wounded, but that blow wasn't a mere scratch either. Inglis rushed to her side, only to be blocked by the beast. It arched its back, threatening to stop her.

"What is this?!" Inglis gasped, staring at several of the creatures. *Summoned monsters, formed of magic or something like it,* she surmised.

Eris grit her teeth in anger. She seemed to recognize the beasts. "Why?! What are you thinking?! Show yourself, Leon!"

"Wait, Leon did that?!"

"Hey. Looks like you figured me out." Leon stepped out of the villa's shadows, a smile on his face. He was wearing the same uniform from earlier at the banquet but with the addition of a pair of gauntlets with indigo spikes.

*Is that his Artifact?*

"Thanks, Inglis! Your distraction gave me just the chance I needed. If I took on Eris straight-up, one of us would have to be hauled off in a cart."

"I thought you were better than this. Are you turning traitor?! You, a holy knight?!"

"Sure looks like it, doesn't it?"

"Leon! Weren't you just saying we had to lick Highlander boots if necessary?! Was that some kind of joke?!" Inglis yelled. *He just tried to stop me from causing any more trouble with Highland. Was that his way of getting closer to Rahl himself?*

## Chapter V: Inglis, Age 12 (Part 2)

"Of course it was! That's too much to ask, even for a holy knight. I'm willing to lay down my life to defend this country and its people."

"So why? Isn't Eris your comrade-in-arms?!"

Leon paused, thinking over his words. "Was. I think I've burned that bridge. You see what's going on, don't you? If I sat by, I'd be serving you up to the Highlander on a platter. That's no way to honor my oath as a holy knight, but there's nothing I can do to stop their ravages. And it tears me up inside! That paradox makes me sick!"

"So you're fighting for justice. How unexpectedly straightforward."

Leon gawked at Inglis. "Not words I expected to hear from a little girl. Just what have you seen in your short life?"

"Without Highland, we can't survive down here!" Eris insisted. "Without Artifacts, we'll die to the magicite beasts! It's just something we have to endure to survive!" The anger on her face had turned to resentment and regret.

"So you just want to give up? I don't. I don't want to give in to the magicite beasts *or* the Highlanders."

"Then what other choice is there?" Inglis asked. *Eris's argument makes sense, but...*

"Inglis, have you heard of the Steelblood Front?" Leon asked.

"No?"

Ymir was far-removed from other cities, and Inglis had paid more attention to her own training than politics. She supposed there was still a lot she didn't know about the world.

Eris was the first to reply. "They're an anti-Highland guerrilla army. They've been getting stronger recently, interfering with operations against the magicite beasts, and I've even heard Highland has destroyed some other cities for assassinating Highlanders. We'd be better off without them! They're just making problems worse!"

"Yeah, that's what the Highlanders have to say about it. But as for us... For us, we're gonna drag Highland down to earth, even if we need to forge our own blood into the steel to make the chains. You understand what that means, right, Inglis?"

"You want to take down Highland first, capture their technology, and spread it across the surface? That way each country would be able to create its own Artifacts and defend itself."

"Clever girl! That's exactly it. No more need to bow and scrape for those damned Highlanders. Sounds perfect, doesn't it? Steelblood has always wanted more good comrades, and this whole mess has convinced me I'm one."

Eris was aghast. "You're underestimating Highland! That would start a war, and there's no way you'd win! Do you realize how much suffering you'd cause?!"

"That's why we need to build up our forces! That's why I want to take you to them. Getting our hands on a hieral menace, the ultimate Artifact, may just be what we need to start cranking out our own!"

"No way! I'm not going along with a plan that will get that many people killed!" Eris leveled her swords, as much to reassure herself as to intimidate Leon.

"How about you, Inglis? Will you be a thug for the Highlanders, or will you be your own woman?"

"No thanks." Inglis declined after a moment's pause.

"Why not? Do you only care about the status quo like Eris?"

"That's not it. If we work together with Eris, we can—"

"C'mon! You're strong. Imagine what you could do with your talent!" Leon insisted, his rabble-rousing getting all the more passionate.

"Just what are—?!" Eris exclaimed, stunned.

"I understand what you mean. But I'm done with throwing my strength into ideology," Inglis declared.

Inglis had already lived that life once before. If she fought for a cause, it would take over her life, which could keep her off the front lines. That wasn't how Inglis Eucus wanted to live!

She fixed a stare Leon's way. "So if you want Eris, you're going to have to go through me."

"I caught only a little bit of your fight earlier, but I know you're

## Chapter V: Inglis, Age 12 (Part 2)

strong," Leon admitted. "Way stronger than you look, so I'm not gonna hold back! Haaah!"

He clanged his Artifact gauntlets together. A hieral menace was only for protecting one's country against the strongest magicite beasts. For other fights, Leon preferred this Artifact. The higher-class Artifact weapons weren't just for slashing, thrusting, and bashing; they were capable of special powers thought of as gifts from heaven. Just what form these 'gifts' took varied by weapon, but for Leon's, it allowed him to summon lightning beasts.

How many there were, and how powerful they were, depended on the wielder. These were in the hands of a holy knight with a special-class rune, though—Leon would be formidable.

Sparks flew toward the ground from the gauntlets as they crashed together, turning to howling lightning beasts as they landed. There had to be at least twenty—no, more than thirty of them surrounding Inglis. It was an impressive, almost blinding, sight.

"One, two, heel! The others—sic!" Leon rushed toward Eris, two lightning beasts at his side.

Eris readied her blades for a counterattack. She and Leon may have been evenly matched alone, but now, she was outnumbered. On top of that, she was already injured.

Inglis didn't think Leon wanted to kill Eris—she wasn't even sure that a hieral menace could die like a human. However, he clearly intended to neutralize her and take her away.

*And if that's what he's after, I'll stop him!* Inglis turned to face the remaining lightning beasts.

*Grrrrr!*
*Hisssss!*
*Awooooo!*

But first, she would need to get through them.
*Sounds fun! I wanted to see a holy knight's gift up close anyway!*

"Haaah!" She swung her fist at the nearest beast, aiming for it perfectly.

But before her strike could connect, a sword swung out of nowhere, slicing through the beast. It belonged to Eris.

The beast cried in pain before exploding in a flash of light just like the one that had struck Eris before. Inglis had scant warning to get back, so she managed to escape only lightly scorched. A direct hit would've hurt far worse.

"Be careful! If we hit them with a strong attack, they'll explode! Keep your distance. Don't dive in!" Eris called to Inglis, who no doubt was less familiar with them.

"Got it!"

But how did Eris slash at it from that far away? Perhaps hieral menaces had gifts too.

*She didn't try that on me. That hurts.*

Inglis asked, "Can you try that on me later?"

"No way! I'm not as bloodthirsty as you!"

Shot down.

At any rate, Eris had told her what she needed to know. If she took the beasts down with a melee attack, she'd be caught up in their explosion. Meaning, she needed to fight from a safe distance.

"Anyway, thanks for the info, Eris. I'll keep it in mind!"

"Ha ha. Don't expect that from me often, but it's fun to show you one of the tricks up my sleeve. Guess I run a bit hot and cold."

"Would you two just shut up?!" Leon interjected, to no one's notice.

"Oh, I see. Hang on, I'm coming for you!" Inglis clenched her fists and focused. "Haaaaaaaaah!"

Her body was covered with a sheen of light and a chilly sensation; she was weaving raw aether. Neither Eris nor Leon knew what that meant. To them, unable to sense aether, it was just a glow. Neither showed any surprise, but they would soon.

Wrapped in light, Inglis made straight for the nearest lightning beast

## Chapter V: Inglis, Age 12 (Part 2)

far faster than she had before, turning her momentum into a roundhouse kick.

The beast yelped in shock, proof that the kick had struck home.

"You idiot! I just told you—" The explosion cut off Eris.

The ball of energy swallowed Inglis, just for her to emerge completely unharmed. Unshaken. Not even stirred. She stood there as if nothing had happened.

Eris gasped, forgetting the fight for a moment. "What the—?!"

"How the hell?!" Leon's hands hung at his sides in shock, too.

"Next!" Inglis took lightning beast after lightning beast down with her bare hands. Even as their explosions wrapped around her, destroying the neatly manicured line of trees, she was unharmed. More and more of the beasts fell, unable to stop her advance.

"Thanks, Eris! You gave me an idea! If I can't avoid their counterattack since I'm fighting them at close range, I just have to strengthen myself until it doesn't hurt me!"

"That's not what I meant! I wanted you to use ranged attacks!"

As they spoke, Inglis had already taken down half of the beasts. Her movements were too fast, too precise, for either the hieral menace or the holy knight to follow. Eris hadn't shown her full power when she and Inglis had fought, but apparently neither had her opponent, whose abilities were far greater. It sent a shiver down Eris's spine. This adorable little girl—did she somehow have power that could shake the foundations of the world?

"I'm faster!" Inglis shouted as waves of aether twisted around her.

This move was Aether Shell, if she had to give it a name. The waves formed a defensive barrier, one that could completely nullify the lightning beasts' explosions. This technique was more than purely defensive; it enhanced her body, making her stronger.

Divine knights were half-human, half-god, and this applied to them physically, not just theologically. They possessed power far greater than an average human. As they grew to maturity, this became even more obvious. The waves of aether around Inglis amped that further. The results were inevitable.

"Haaaah!" Inglis's fist smashed into the last lightning beast, and though it twisted to deliver a return blow, the barrier blocked that attack completely. Inglis smoothly strode onward to Eris and stood by her side. "Sorry to keep you waiting."

"Who taught you your manners? Asking me not to hold back when you were holding back yourself!"

"That's not true."

If Aether Shell had a flaw, it was that it couldn't be maintained for long. As it faded, so would her strength. It was a last-ditch effort. Perhaps, as she grew, she'd be able to hold the aether in place longer, keep its effects through an extended fight—but that all came down to training.

Leon shrugged in resignation. "You really are a handful. Not even that many were enough to hold you back?"

If Inglis was stronger than even a holy knight or a hieral menace...

"Even me and Eris together would probably have a hard time taking you on. I bet you'd be able to handle a Prismer yourself," he acknowledged.

"Yes. I've been training to do exactly that."

"What?! Are you serious?!"

"But of course."

"Ha ha ha! Amazing! You dream big, kid. But whatever you've got planned for the future, I bet you've got a weakness now. Like, maybe... you can't keep up that power for long?"

*Smart one, isn't he?* Inglis mused. *He may play the fool, but he's got a sharp mind and strong convictions. If I'd met him in my past life, I may have taken him on as a close adviser.*

"So what if I can't?" she shot back.

"It means I can wear you down! I've got plenty left where that came from!" Leon again moved his gauntlets to summon the lightning beasts. The clash of steel on steel rang through the air.

Yet no beasts came.

"Wha...?!"

"I won't let you do that," Inglis interjected.

She'd delivered a swift kick before his fists could meet. The noise wasn't the clash of gauntlets against each other but the gauntlets clashing with Inglis's greave.

Inglis had confirmed he could use his gift only when the gauntlets struck together. She had guessed as much from seeing him before, but now she was certain.

"S-Seriously?" Leon hadn't even seen it happening. By the time he focused, his vision was full of a dented greave and a well-formed thigh.

"Oh, and it's rude to stare at a lady's legs."

"C'mon! You shoved your leg right in my face!" Leon leaped backward, hoping to keep his distance.

"I told you, no." Inglis followed his movements exactly, catching him by the wrists and holding him still.

"Ngh...!"

"Hi-yah!" Inglis slammed her foot into Leon's gut, the force of the impact leaving him hanging in the air for a moment.

"Gah?!" Leon slumped onto the ground.

Inglis moved to make sure he was unconscious, but suddenly another fighter entered the ring. The walls of the villa crumbled, accompanied by a thundering roar.

"Eeek!" A girl leaped away from the collapsing wall—Rafinha.

"Rani?!" Inglis's eyes reflexively snapped to her as she called her name. Rafinha wasn't the only thing that came flying from the rubble, though.

"Grrraaahhh!"

Along with her, there was a gigantic humanoid *thing*. Almost definitely what had collapsed the wall. Its upper body was swollen and bloated with muscle, its thick hide studded on its brow, neck, and back with gems. Aqua, ultramarine, gold, black...

"Is that a magicite beast?!" Inglis shouted in surprise.

But there hadn't been any signs of Prism Flow! This one was humanoid too. Inglis had never seen one like it before.

She snapped back to the immediate danger. "No, wait! Rani!"

There would be time to think later. Right now, Inglis needed to protect Rafinha. That was the one oath for others' sakes that Inglis Eucus had sworn.

"Graaahhh!"

The humanoid magicite beast slammed its fist down toward Rani, who shrieked in terror.

"Eek!"

"I won't let you hurt her! Haaah!"

Inglis quickly moved into the path of the swing, winding up her own punch. By weight or force alone, the beast easily had the upper hand, but that didn't guarantee it victory. The force of Inglis's attack sent it stumbling back until it struck the walls of the villa.

"Rani! Are you okay?!"

"Th-Thanks, Chris."

"What are you doing here?" Inglis figured Rafinha must have been so insistent that not even Duke Bilford could stop her.

"I don't care that they didn't want me to come. I can't let you go into this alone! So I thought I'd take care of Rahl myself, but...something's not right!"

"What do you mean?"

"I was hiding, waiting to see what would happen. Then he suddenly hunched over in pain and transformed into that!" Rafinha gestured at the magicite beast.

"What?! You're saying that's Rahl?!"

"It is! I watched him turn into that!"

"Inglissssss!" The beast that had been Rahl hissed her name as it drew close.

## Chapter V: Inglis, Age 12 (Part 2)

"It knows my name?!" Inglis gasped. "It *must* be Rahl, but how?! I've never heard of the Prism Flow affecting humans!"

The Prism Flow just didn't affect humans. That was well-known, not in the least by people who'd been caught in it and lived to tell the tale. Inglis didn't expect there to be any exceptions.

"I swear it's him! Is this my fault, Chris? Did I do something?"

"Don't worry," Leon said, climbing to his feet. He had resummoned his lightning beasts, which formed a menacing wall around him. "It's not your fault, Rafinha. Just before you got here, I gave him a dose of Prism Powder. It's a concentrated version of the Prism Flow. The Steelbloods were more than happy to hook me up with some. It doesn't affect humans much, but Highlanders—well, you see what happened. We may be used to the flow down here, but still. It's not something you wanna mess with. At this point, he's gone. He's nothing more than a beast." Leon's words were full of loathing as he hunched his shoulders in disgust.

Eris asked, "Isn't there some kind of way to turn him back? There has to be!"

"You want to help this guy, Eris? The only way to help him is to put him out of his misery."

"But we can't just kill a Highlander!" Eris protested.

"Climb down from your damn ivory tower for once. You know there's no way to turn him back. If there was, we'd just use it on the magicite beasts to begin with and solve our problems that way!"

Eris grit her teeth. "Ugh…"

"Blame it all on me!" Leon continued. "A Steelblood spy in your midst—there's your excuse! Just let me make my escape. I'm not sure my ego could take it if I got nabbed right away after all this plotting!"

"Ah! Wait!"

"Explode!" he commanded.

The lightning beasts exploded in a blinding flash of light.

"Gah!"

"Shoot, he got away!"

By the time Inglis and Eris could see again, Leon was long gone.

The best case would have been to drag him in chains before the king to confess his crimes. Still, they couldn't ignore Rahl, now a beast in front of them. Pursuing Leon would have to be left for later. Worst case, Eris could explain what had happened here. The word of a hieral menace would surely carry some weight, even if it wasn't as good as presenting the culprit.

"Ingliiisssss!"

The beast's roar almost sounded like a plea to ease his suffering. It would be hard to argue that Rahl wasn't a profoundly twisted individual who'd gotten what he deserved. All the same, though, he was pitiful.

Inglis stood before the beast. "We go back a long way. I'm going to make sure you can rest in peace. Now, the question is how…"

He was gigantic and probably just as tough as his size implied. A quick blast would put him out of his misery, but Inglis feared unleashing that would seriously damage everything nearby. The villa was already a wreck, so she wasn't worried about that in particular, but she was concerned about the wreckage spreading further.

She had to get him out of town and beat him there, but that would leave a trail of rubble in his wake. She didn't want to put the people of Ymir in danger.

After some more thinking, she exclaimed, "All right!"

*I've got it!*

"Inglisssss!"

The beast swung a massive fist toward Inglis, who leaped away.

She could have tanked it or tried to counter, but dodging let her gain some distance. Inglis stretched forward as she landed. She would use her momentum at that range to keep moving! Just then, she heard a deep voice call out.

Duke Bilford bellowed, "Rafinha! Inglis! I can't just leave this all to you two! What are you doing, you accursed Highlander?!"

Voices called out over the sound of armored boots approaching. "Rafinha! Inglis! We're here to help!"

"Father! Ada! You came? But why?!" Rafinha cried, but her tone suggested she was not as displeased about the backup as she was trying to sound.

"Rafinha! Inglis! Are you okay? Wait, why is there a magicite beast?!" Ada barked orders to her knights. "Don't let it out of the villa! Spread out and attack!"

"Wait! It's a tough one! Don't let it get close to you!" Inglis warned. "I'll be fine, Eris is here to help!"

"Huh? Me? I mean, I am, but against something like that—"

As Eris sputtered in confusion, Inglis pulled her away. "We're going in!"

"O-Okay!"

The two charged toward Rahl at full speed. Inglis may have been a bit rough with her, but Eris was, after all, a hieral menace. She could keep up. Rahl swung a fist to sweep them away, but they were too fast for it to connect.

"On my mark, kick!" Inglis instructed.

"Got it!"

"Haaaaaah!"

Inglis and Eris both yelled, putting their all into kicks aimed at Rahl's abdomen. The power behind their blows was made clear by the sickening *thwack!* as he soared into the air, sailing like an arrow over the walls of Ymir before landing in the outskirts. This was the best, fastest way to get him out of the city while preventing any damage.

"A-Amazing!" Duke Bilford and his knights gasped in awe.

"Wow! You're amazing, Eris!" Inglis clapped.

"What are you talking about? There's no way I could have—"

Inglis quietly hushed her. "Shhh! Play along!"

Inglis had managed to conceal her true power from everyone but Rafinha, but her swordfighting had already gained her quite the reputation. She didn't want to invite further questions or, even worse, the responsibility of protecting Ymir herself. How would she set off to find stronger foes with that on her back? If she was going to master the blade, she needed fewer things holding her down. That included great expectations of her. That was how she'd ended up a hero-king to begin with.

"O-Okay." Eris nodded.

"Time to finish him off, then! Let's go, Rani!" Inglis called.

"Sure, Chris!"

Inglis took Eris's and Rafinha's hands, and they were gone in a flash, running through the streets of Ymir to the outer walls. It was late at night, and the gates were closed, so they jumped over the walls. It was an easy feat for Eris, but it was one that required a quick piggyback ride for Rafinha.

Rahl was a bit scratched up, but he could still rise to his feet and attempt to tear a hole through the walls.

"Looks like he's still got some fight left in him!" Rafinha said. "What a tough guy! I can't believe that after that kick from you and Eris—"

"That was pretty much all Inglis. She's ridiculous."

"Wow! You're amazing, Chris! Even a hieral menace has good things to say about you!"

"Aha ha ha. Let's worry about that later. Remember, normal attacks don't work against magicite beasts."

"I can't really call a kick like that normal. You saw how he went flying," Eris said.

"Sure, but it's a question of what kind of power's behind it, not how much strength you put into it," Inglis replied.

Normal attacks, or even a crash landing like that, didn't really hurt magicite beasts. The power of an Artifact was necessary to put them down.

Inglis had used Aether Shell for its protective barrier and boosted physical capabilities, but she hadn't used aether to power the attack specifically. While that may have been enough to handle a weaker magicite beast, Rahl was something else. Inglis had to break him, not merely bruise him. She needed one decisive, fatal blow.

"Eris, does Rahl measure up to a Prismer?"

## Chapter V: Inglis, Age 12 (Part 2)

After a pause, Eris replied, "No. As tough as he is, he's not that tough. It's like comparing an adult to a child."

"I see. So if this doesn't work on him, it definitely won't work on a Prismer. Let me give it a try anyway. Watch this, Rani."

Inglis faced down Rahl as he advanced, her right palm thrust forth. Beams swirled around her hand as the aether condensed, kicking up a whirlwind that sent her hair to and fro. Glimmering cold light formed into a sphere of pure aether, one large enough to swallow even Rahl whole. This was Aether Strike, which she'd been able to use even as a baby. Now it had twelve more years of training behind it, and it was far more powerful.

*Here's my chance to see just how far I've come!*

Spotting Inglis again, Rahl lurched to his feet and stumbled toward her. "Innngliiisssss!"

"Goodbye, Rahl..."

Inglis unleashed her Aether Strike.

*Blammmmmm!*

A ball of light larger than ever before shot toward him, carving through the terrain as it homed in before swallowing the beast and reducing him to a cloud of pale-white ash.

In the end, Rahl was defanged and left scattered to the winds.

"W-Wow..." Eris muttered.

Rafinha jumped for joy. "Great job, Chris! I knew you could do it!"

"Phew..." Inglis exhaled. "That wore me out."

She had used too much aether, and a wave of exhaustion dragged her down to the ground. She still needed more training. Her growing body lacked endurance.

Rafinha and Eris rushed to her side.

"Chris!"

"Are you okay?"

"You were right, Rani." Inglis smiled weakly at Rafinha.

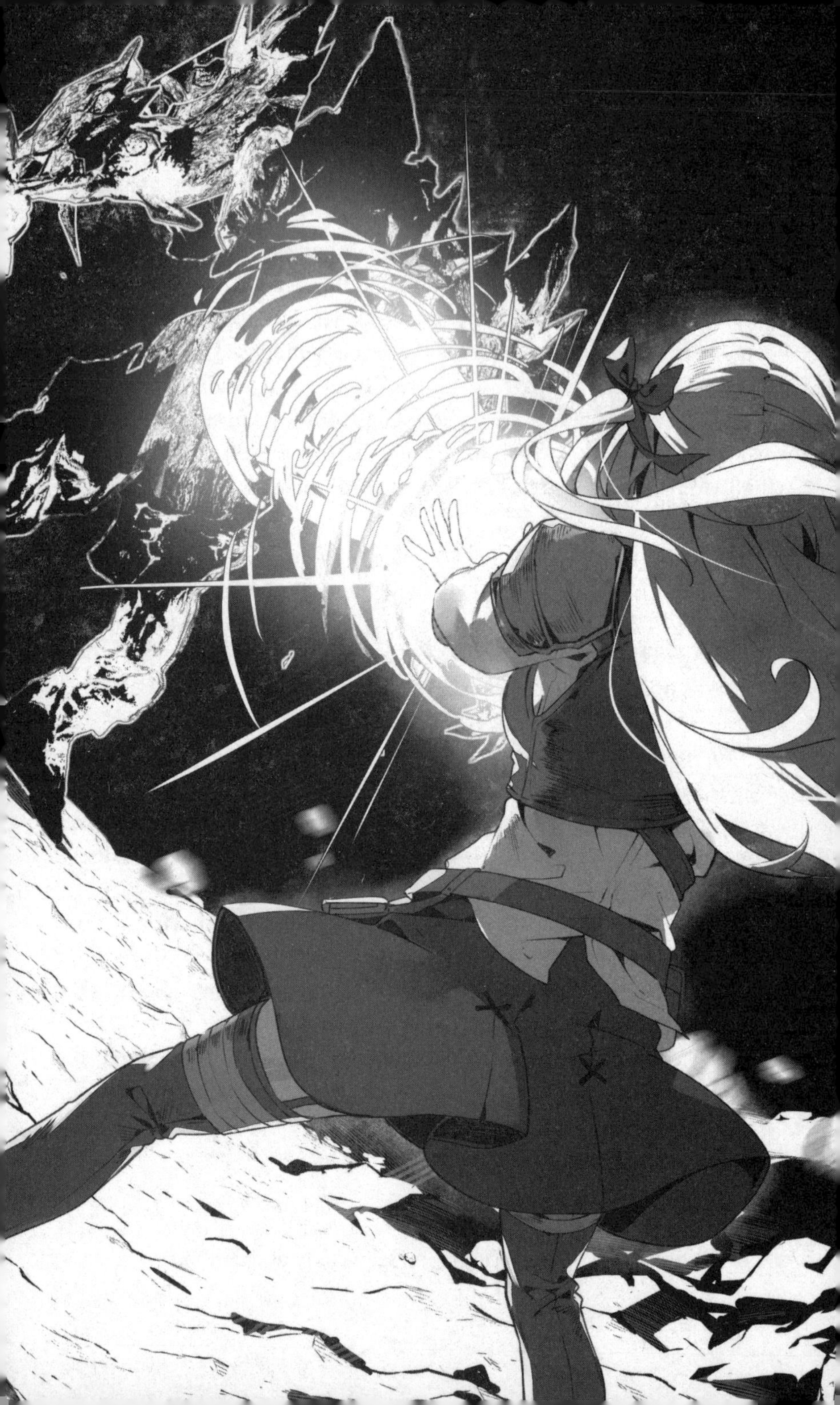

## Chapter V: Inglis, Age 12 (Part 2)

"Huh? What do you mean?"

"When we made our wishes on Highland. Today I had some really satisfying fights."

"You're still thinking about that? I told you it'd be a real mess if that wish came true..."

"Ha ha. You're not wrong about that, but in the end we both got what we wished for."

"It's a good thing you were here," Eris said. "Imagine if I'd been taken by the Steelbloods, and left unable to stop that beast as it rampaged through the city? This could have been far worse."

"That's kind of you to say."

"When I return to the capital, I'll report that this was all part of Leon's plan to turn traitor. Rafael will back me up. I'll try to make sure you don't take any of the blame. Can't make any guarantees, though."

"Thanks! One other thing. Can you play down my involvement and make it seem like you fought Rahl instead?"

"If you'd rather it that way, that's fine by me. But you *will* owe me one." Eris smiled as she reached her hand out to Inglis.

"Got it." Taking Eris's hand, Inglis pulled herself to her feet. As she did, she could see Duke Bilford and his knights approaching swiftly.

◆ ◇ ◆

Early the next morning, leaving the manhunt for Leon to Ymir's knights, Eris set off for the capital. Inglis followed to see her off, and when they were alone together, she had one more question.

"Can I ask you one thing, Eris?"

"What?"

"Why did you get angry when Leon introduced us to you at the banquet?"

It was obvious to Inglis, after fighting alongside Eris, that how she'd acted then was out of the ordinary. Eris normally had more of a level head.

Eris hesitated. "I'm sorry. You might realize why someday, but I don't want to tell you." She took in a breath. "And I hope you don't ever find out."

"I see. Sorry for asking something so personal."

"Don't worry about it. I should get going— Wait, you said you wanted to take on a Prismer by yourself, right? Do your best. I'll be cheering you on."

"Thank you."

"Until we meet again."

"Someday."

Sent off with a smile, Eris departed from Ymir.

# Chapter VI: Inglis, Age 15— Journey to the Capital

Three years had passed since the incident in Ymir, during which the city under Bilford's rule had endured the deaths of Lord Shiony and Rahl the Highlander. Another inspector had arrived from the capital shortly afterward, this time without a Highlander in tow, and judged Ymir blameless for what had happened. It was thanks to the hard work of Eris and Rafael that the inspector had made such a decision.

Inglis's training regimen grew even more intense over those three years, and Rafinha often joined her, honing her skills with the bow.

At the age of fifteen, their lives would change.

A covered wagon waited beside the gates of Ymir. Inglis and Rafinha were waiting next to it as their families, the knights, and the townspeople wished them fond farewells.

The duke proffered fatherly advice. "Stay well, Rafinha. Don't get into any fights with Rafael. And remember to thank Lady Eris for all she's done for us."

"Of course, father. I'll write as soon as I arrive," she replied. "I'm not sure if Rafael is just too busy to write or if he's choosing not to, but I'll keep in touch."

As Rafinha smiled from her father's embrace, Inglis thought of how much her cousin had grown. *She's turning into a woman, but she still has that upbeat personality. She's so striking that she keeps turning my head before I realize it.*

At fifteen years old, Rafinha had been accepted as a cadet at the knights' academy. Today was the day she departed for the capital.

She wouldn't be alone, though—Inglis was joining her. As a Runeless, she was disqualified from full knighthood but not from life as a squire. Thus, she was allowed to train at the academy.

Training for knights and squires differed in the fine details, but the theoretical lectures and the practical exercises were largely the same. Plus, as roommates, their daily life wouldn't change much at all.

"Inglis, please take good care of Rafinha," the duke said.

"Of course."

As Inglis nodded, the duke leaned in and whispered, "And, of course, deal with any bad influences on her. She's a curious girl—sometimes a bit *too* curious."

"Of course, Your Grace." Inglis was in full agreement about the dangers of boyfriends. After all, Rafinha may have been Duke Bilford's daughter, but she was also something like a granddaughter to Inglis.

He added, "Though I'm sure you're more likely to draw their attention yourself."

Rafinha turned heads, but Inglis at this point drew outright stares. Her platinum blonde hair shimmered like the summer moon, her ruby-red eyes gleamed like jewels, and she was well into her growth spurt. Just as when she was twelve, she looked older than her actual age. People mistook her for fourteen or fifteen years old then, and now at fifteen she could be mistaken for eighteen. Moreover, she was beautiful from head to toe.

After concluding his farewell to his daughter, the duke turned to his captain of the knights. "I can only imagine what worries are going through your mind, Luke."

### Chapter VI: Inglis, Age 15—Journey to the Capital

"Yes, it's quite the problem," Inglis's father said. "She's such a beauty it's awkward to go anywhere with her."

"Oh, don't be such a fuddy-duddy! I'm sure she'll be a wonderful duchess someday!" Rafinha beamed.

"Mm. Even a wallflower like Rafael is sure to notice her," the duke said.

Luke agreed. "Which means a bright future for Ymir. At least, if Rafael is so inclined."

"Yeah, totally! I'm sure she'll make an impression!" Rafinha gave voice to the spreading excitement. It seemed like everyone was in agreement about where Inglis should set her sights.

"Oh no," Inglis reflexively cut in. "Calm down, everyone."

*Or at least ask my opinion first!* Inglis couldn't help but think resentfully. *The problem isn't Rafael himself—it's that he's a guy. I don't even want to think about it. My tastes haven't changed, so I'd rather you were trying to set me up with a woman, honestly.*

She cleared her throat. "I am, of course, Rani's squire. I have no intention of wasting a single moment of my study."

Two voices cut through the chatter.

"Rafinha!"

"Inglis!"

Irina and Serena called out to their daughters as they approached breathlessly, carrying large bundles under their arms.

Rafinha and Inglis responded happily in turn.

"Mother!"

"Mom!"

The two mothers' words overlapped. "Sorry to keep you waiting! We packed you lunch!"

Each had put together a basket that would feed a grown man for three days. It was a prodigious amount of food, but it was not an unusual sight for Inglis or Rafinha, both of whom had equally enormous appetites to match. Rafael, Serena, and Irina were all big eaters too. Perhaps the trait was genetic. When the extended families ate together, it wasn't uncommon for the duke and Luke to be amazed by how much their households could fit in their stomachs.

"Thank you!" Inglis and Rafinha replied with smiles as their mothers came in for teary embraces.

Irina bid her daughter farewell. "Take care, sweetie. And remember, Chris will be there for you."

"I know you two will be each other's rocks," Serena said. "Remember—no matter how tough things get, never give up."

Inglis thought back to her past life, born in a poor farming village and orphaned at eight. Yet as Inglis Eucus, she had spent fifteen years with loving parents and wide-open horizons; she had wanted for nothing in this childhood.

Now, though, it was time to set out beyond her home comforts and train herself further in battle. The capital was a crossroads for people and information alike, and she might well encounter a worthy foe there. Her first step would be gathering that information, though. If the kingdom was in danger, leaders could mobilize her as a cadet without her having to lift a finger. That would be something to look forward to! As grateful as she was to her parents, it was time to leave Ymir and chase that opportunity.

"We're off, then!" Inglis announced.

Rafinha chimed in, "Thank you for everything! Stay well!"

The crowd waved as the wagon's wheels creaked into motion. Inglis took the reins, Rafinha seated at her side. As Duke Bilford and Serena faded from sight, she began to sniffle, the farewells pulling at her heart. Tears welled up in her eyes.

"Don't cry, Rani. Our real challenges begin here." Inglis wiped her eyes with a fingertip.

"Yeah… You're right. I know I'll be fine if you're here with me. All right, then, let's have lunch. ♪" Rafinha produced the lunches from the wagon bed. "I'm starving!"

"No fair! I have to hold the reins!"

## Chapter VI: Inglis, Age 15—Journey to the Capital

"Don't worry. I'll feed you. ♪" Rafinha pressed the corner of a sandwich into Inglis's mouth.

"Fhnkf... Mmmm, vhf'ff gwwf..."

The sandwich would be her last taste of home for a long time. Better to savor it as much as possible.

As they enjoyed their meal, Ymir faded into the distance...

# Chapter VII: Inglis, Age 15—The City Ruled by Highlanders (Part 1)

Ten or so days had passed since Inglis had left her hometown, Ymir. The journey from Ymir to Chiral, the capital, was expected to take just under a month, so she and Rafinha were a third of the way to their destination—or so one might assume.

"Mmmm! This is great! ♪ I love traveling. You get to go to so many places and try so much food!"

The town of Nova, their current location, was set in the foothills of a nearby mountain, where wild greens and fruits were abundant. Rafinha shoveled a slice of raspberry pie, laden with decadent jam and entire berries, into her mouth with a satisfied smile.

The table she shared with Inglis was decked with pastries made from the famous local raspberries, and she'd already eaten enough for several grown men. Other tables may have been casting over the occasional stare of awe, but both girls were well used to that.

"Are you sure you're not eating too much, Rani?"

"You've had just as much as I had."

Inglis was indeed rapidly making her way through the food as fast as Rafinha was. No plate was left uncleaned as the two danced through a sugar-sweet daydream. *In my past life, I was a big eater, but never like this. I never liked sweets either. Now I do. Is it because I was reborn as a* woman? I guess in any case it's another way to live life differently. I'd never have tried dressing up or eating things like this before.

"Yeah, but… Really, we'll be in trouble."

"What kind of trouble?"

"Our budget. If we don't eat normal portions, our money will never last until Chiral."

"Whaaat?! So we won't be able to try any of the delicious things waiting for us?"

"That's right. That's why I said we're eating too much."

"So then why don't we just take the most direct route?"

"Absolutely not! We need to visit Ahlemin first."

Inglis was absolutely insistent on this detour and had planned for it in her initial budget. This city had a landmark she desperately wanted to see: the huge corpse of a Prismer, slain by a holy knight and hieral menace team over fifty years before. She hoped to experience a little bit of the power of such a monster. Would that even work? She wasn't sure, but she was equally unsure it would be fruitless, so why not try anyway?

"That's why we need to cut back," Inglis continued. "This is our last fancy—"

"No way!" Rafinha interrupted. "That's no fun at all! When are we ever going to have a chance like this again?"

"Do you have any better ideas, then?"

"If it's money we need, why not just earn it on the way? We have plenty of time before we're supposed to arrive, right?"

"Well… Yeah, we have some leeway," Inglis acquiesced. She knew she was easy on Rafinha, who was like the granddaughter she'd never had, so it was easy to tolerate her whims. Like usual, she found herself going along with what Rafinha wanted.

"All right, then! It's a working holiday, eating our way across the country! She who will not work shall not eat! That should be no problem, though. We've got the skills to earn far more than we were given for the trip."

## Chapter VII: Inglis, Age 15—The City Ruled by Highlanders (Part 1)

"Yeah. So I guess when we get to the next—"

Before Inglis could even finish her sentence, Rafinha, always quick on her feet, had flagged the waitress down. "Excuse me, waitress!"

"Um, Rani..."

"Yes? What can I get you?" the waitress asked.

"Three more slices of raspberry pie! ♪" Rafinha swiftly replied.

"Okay! I'll have that right out!"

Inglis tried to get her back on track. "C'mon, Rani."

"Wait, sorry, one more thing. Do you happen to know where we'd find work in this town? Something where we can really show off—and earn—what we're worth!" Rafinha showed her hand to the waitress.

"Oh my! So you've a Rune?"

"Yes. An Artifact too!" The bow Rafinha carried was such an object, and it was well-suited to her upper-class Rune. The Artifact had not been in the armories of Ymir, and Duke Bilford had worked hard to acquire the new item for his daughter. With this bow in her hands, none of the knights—or the magicite beasts they'd encountered for that matter—had been a match.

"So young and yet already a knight. Incredible!"

"Well, actually, we're on our way to the knights' academy, but..."

"In any case, if you're looking for that kind of work, the local lord is hiring knights and mercenaries. Why not see him? I'm sure he'd be happy to have you lend a hand against the magicite beasts."

"That's perfect! Right, Chris?" Rafinha's eyes were gleaming.

"I guess, but... You say he's recruiting? What happened to his old forces?" Inglis pressed the waitress for details.

"He drove the old lord's lot out when he took power. Thanks to that, life around here has improved, and the taxes have gone down. But it does mean he's a bit pressed for a few blades. Not enough to lower his standards, though."

"So he cleaned house, then?"

"Well, more like he had no connection to the old lord at all," the waitress explained plainly. "The old nobility was abolished, and we came under direct administration by the Highlanders. Our new lord is one of them."

"A Highlander?!" Both Inglis and Rafinha were shocked.

"My apologies—I meant we came under the king's direct control, but we're overseen by a Highlander. Sorry, I'm still not excited about that part."

"...Yeah, it's probably best to leave it at that."

Regardless of the actual forces at work, how could a king maintain his authority if he couldn't claim to have maintained his borders? If the pretext for the change was to remove an unpopular lord, the entire process could be presented as the failings of the previous lord rather than of the king—even if the reality was that he couldn't resist the Highlander's demands.

Still, what was the advantage for the Highlanders? Colonization? But why would a Highlander, nestled in the bosom of privilege, choose to move to the surface? Was Nova a base from which to deliver crops and other resources? Perhaps it was less expensive to operate than the Artifact-for-offerings trade? Overseeing the city's rule in-person had its own risks, though.

If nothing else, it was sure to fan the flames of anti-Highlander sentiment and drive an increase in Steelblood Front activity. Or was their military supremacy so mighty that no opposition could be made?

Highland supplied hieral menaces, Artifacts beyond compare; surely they had plans for how to defeat them as well. That meant Highland might be forced to show a secret weapon if a team of a holy knight and a hieral menace arose in opposition to them. That idea, and how she might respond, fascinated Inglis.

"So we won't be in any danger meeting him?" Rafinha asked.

Rahl was the only Highlander the pair had met before, and Inglis understood Rafinha's trepidation about meeting another.

"No," the waitress replied. "Like I said, things have only improved here since he arrived. Well, mostly improved. Sales have gone down, but

## Chapter VII: Inglis, Age 15—The City Ruled by Highlanders (Part 1)

what can I do? At night, we're a bar—in a town with fewer drunk soldiers."

"I see…"

"But really, he's not a bad man. He cares for orphans and the ill in his manor. When I saw that, I was relieved that we finally had a good lord." The waitress smiled.

"I guess there are good Highlanders too?" Rafinha said, but she sounded unconvinced as she cast a hesitant glance toward Inglis.

"Maybe. Why don't we go see for ourselves?" Inglis said. She thought this would be a good opportunity to learn more about Highland—for herself but especially for Rafinha.

"We'll do that, then! But not before one more slice of raspberry pie!"

"Okay."

After finishing their meal, they set off for the local manor house.

They easily negotiated a deal. It was practically instantaneous once they showed off Rafinha's Bow of Light Rune and Artifact.

Inglis was, of course, welcome along as her squire but equally expected to demonstrate what she was capable of. Thus, she found herself in the manor's courtyard, facing the burly knight assigned command of the ragtag local forces. He looked like he was in his early twenties, well-muscled but with the air of a calm and confident nobleman rather than an intense fighter.

"I'm Nash. Sorry, but I need to see what you're made of before I send you out to the front lines to get hurt," he said.

"I don't mind. I suppose I understand why you'd be concerned," Inglis replied.

The sparring match would be a simple one with wooden swords.

Rafinha barely stifled a yawn, struggling to hide her boredom as the knights and mercenaries crowded in to watch. "You're wasting your time making Chris prove herself…"

For Inglis, though, this was a great opportunity. All eyes were on her, and she would dispel any illusions the crowd had about her. If anything, she was thankful for this chance. She would put it to good use.

"All right, show me what you've got!" Nash called.

"Very well." Inglis darted in, sweeping aside Nash's wooden sword. He was too slow to respond, and it went flying from his hand.

"Wh—?!"

Before he could recover from the surprise, she slammed her palm into his unguarded belly.

"Gwuh?!" Nash doubled over as he went flying backward.

"Whoaaaa!" Everyone watching rose to their feet, shocked, as Nash smashed butt-first into the ground and tumbled a few times.

A dizzy Nash could only manage to mumble, "I... I think you pass..."

"Ah. Whoops. Guess I went a little too hard! Sorry about that. C'mon, let's get you on your feet."

Inglis had put too much force into her attack, and she felt terrible about that. She rushed to his side, slapping his cheeks to try to bring him back to his senses.

It wasn't long before the situation took a turn for the worse.

A man rushed in, eyes wide in shock. "Big trouble! Magicite beasts!" he cried. "Nash?! Nash! What happened?!"

*Bad timing. Real bad timing.*

Inglis called out, "Uh... T-To the defense!"

At Inglis's shout, the stunned knights came back to their senses.

"A-All right!"

"Yeah, we've gotta hold the magicite beasts off!"

"Let's go! Hurry!"

◆◇◆

Inglis and Rafinha joined the knights' sortie against the magicite beasts. They may have been newcomers, but they were recruits nonetheless, so this was their job to deal with too.

Nova's walls surrounding the city were weak, basically nothing more than stone fences as tall as the average adult. This was quite different from

## Chapter VII: Inglis, Age 15—The City Ruled by Highlanders (Part 1)

the ring around Ymir, which was thrice as tall and wide enough for forces to patrol on the walkway. It would be supremely difficult to mount a defense from the walls.

On the other hand, the lord's manor here was of far stouter construction than the castle the Bilfords of Ymir called home. Generations of local gentry must have paid special attention to the manor. Occasional heaps of stone and patches of scaffolding indicated there had been recent efforts to reinforce the walls—likely a decision of the new Highlander lord, who'd been described to Inglis and Rafinha as a woman named Cyrene.

Rafinha frowned. "Defending this city is gonna be pretty hard."

"Yeah. We can't hold these walls against a magicite beast," Inglis said. "Our only option is to defeat it first."

Fortunately, no beasts had reached the city proper. Taking the battle outside the walls was the obvious course of action.

"So, what are we up against?" Inglis asked as she scaled the wall to get a better view. For a woman who was able to climb the walls of Ymir without breaking a sweat, it was an easy task, but it still raised the morale of the nearby knights. She continued working through the situation aloud. "Beasts and an insectoid—probably a dragonfly? If I'm right, that one could bypass the wall easily."

Rafinha followed Inglis, surveying the battlefield alongside her. A knight's Artifact wasn't just a weapon; it also enhanced their physical abilities. The higher the Rune's class, the stronger the Artifact and the greater its effects were. The lowest Runes and Artifacts did little to improve the wielder's capabilities. Thanks to Rafinha's powerful Rune, scaling the walls wasn't difficult for her either. If she tried, she'd likely manage it even in Ymir.

Rafinha agreed with Inglis. "Right? We should go out there and—"

"Excuse me!" a knight called down from below. "Do you have a moment?"

"Yes! What do you need?" Inglis answered.

Rafinha chimed in as well. "Is there something we can help you with?"

"We'd like you to take command. Nash is in no condition to fight right now, and none of us have any leadership experience. But you have an upper-class Rune! You can take charge!"

The local knights lacked combat experience. The ruffians previously in Nova had already driven out the battle-hardened knights. Military force was as much a matter of discipline and organization as it was of raw strength. The present knights did not have the latter.

Rafinha, tapped for command, frowned in discomfort. "A-Are you sure? Chris, don't you have any command experience?" She'd fought alongside the knights of Ymir, but she'd never led them. That had been a task for the captain, Luke, and his lieutenant, Ada.

"Better get used to it now. You've got an upper-class Rune, Rani. When you become a full knight, you'll be in command often."

"B-But is it really okay to jump into this as a newbie?"

"Don't worry. I'll give you suggestions. First, have an imposing presence. A calm, cool-headed leader makes for calm, cool-headed troops."

Inglis didn't have any command experience—well, none that anyone else knew of. In her past life, she'd commanded small squads like these to regiments and entire armies. She didn't anticipate this group to be difficult to manage.

"Okay, I think I get it," Rafinha said before turning to the assembled knights. "All right, everyone! Follow me! We'll drive the magicite beasts off!" She brandished her Artifact bow.

"Hurrah!" Cheers of approval rose up from below. It came as no surprise—a maiden like Rafinha would be not only a commander but also a symbol of what they were fighting for.

"S-So... Now what, Chris?"

"Leave it to me." Inglis cleared her own throat and raised her voice. "The humble Inglis Eucus shall convey our leader's commands! Make camp around the gates and await the enemy's approach! If a beast assaults, intercept it and drive it away!"

In other words, she was ordering them to keep watch. The knights whispered confused questions to one another, but Inglis continued.

## Chapter VII: Inglis, Age 15—The City Ruled by Highlanders (Part 1)

"Inglis—that is, I—will charge forth to draw the beasts' attention, and it's when they falter that Rafinha will destroy them with the power of her Artifact! To your positions!"

Making a plan around Rafinha's bow was a safer, swifter choice than solely meeting the foes head-on.

Inglis whispered to her friend. "You know what to do, Rani?"

"What we always do, right? You're just making it sound impressive."

"Exactly. Ready?"

"Yeah."

"Then, Inglis Eucus shall sally forth!" Her voice boomed as she leaped from the walls and advanced on the mass of magicite beasts. There were dozens of foes, yet she charged forth unflinchingly.

"Wh-What is she doing?!"

"Wait! There's too many!"

"Someone stop her!"

Cries of dismay arose from behind Inglis as the knights thought she was sacrificing herself. However, they would soon realize that she was in no danger. Inglis, a one-woman battalion—if not a one-woman army—crashed into a group of magicite beasts.

*Grrrr!*
*Awoooo!*
*Growllll!*

The three beasts, formerly dogs or wolves, made a triangle formation with the leader front and center.

Inglis jumped and stomped the lead beast's left shoulder as she dodged its bite. "Haaaah!" she cried as she swiftly slammed her other foot into the side of its skull, sending it tumbling into its follower.

*Two down.*

The third, last to arrive, rushed in to bite Inglis. She didn't have time to properly evade. Instead, she used the momentum of her kick from a moment ago to twist herself upward, fangs slicing through empty space before sticking into the ground. She ran along the beast's back, leaping into the air again. She had jumped toward the hovering insectoid to draw its attention. It may have once been a dragonfly, but its legs were now long blades akin to scythes.

And now those blades were pointing toward Inglis as it swooped down.

But were they blades, or were they stepping-stones?

Inglis evaded the beast's slashes and landed perfectly on one scythe before leaping nimbly to another. She kept jumping from one to the next until she found her opening.

As the insect continued its attempts to scrape her off, Inglis tumbled forward and smashed the membrane between its head and its body. "Yaaah!"

It let out a roar of pain as it fell to the ground, and a mass of other beasts swarmed toward Inglis. Her plan to draw their attention had succeeded. Simple weapons and bare-handed strikes couldn't defeat magicite beasts, but they sure could draw their attention. Inglis could have defeated them with Aether Strike and Aether Shell, but she couldn't rely on those for long yet, so she reserved those techniques for when they were really necessary.

Besides, an easy win wasn't a satisfying win. She could throw herself into the teeming mass of the enemy with Aether Shell and emerge without a scratch, but it wouldn't have accomplished her goal here. She wanted to practice unarmed combat and get the feel for its momentum in battle; there was no reason to let an opportunity go to waste.

"W-Wow! Look at her goooo!"

"She's so amazing!"

"What a beautiful sight! I can't believe it!"

Inglis had drawn the attention of the knights as much as she had that of the beasts. They were focused solely on her and had even set aside their arms to watch her fight. That fight was otherworldly. *She* was otherworldly. They wondered if it had all been a dream. If it had

## Chapter VII: Inglis, Age 15—The City Ruled by Highlanders (Part 1)

been, the knights hoped not to wake so that they could see more. They were transfixed, their fists clenched, their cheers ragged with anticipation.

Meanwhile, Rafinha made her move, taking a position between the knights and Inglis. She gripped her Artifact bow. From her hand, a bright white arrow of light sprang forth, growing as it gathered energy. Her Artifact needed no physical arrows—a knight worthy of wielding it could create them from pure light as if by magic. This was Rafinha's Gift, one she called "Shiny Flow." It still had its limits, but the longer and harder she drew the bowstring, the more forceful the bolt would be. She got ready to fire.

"Chris! You ready? Here it comes!"

"Yeah, Rani! Go ahead!"

"All right! Here goes!" Rafinha shot over the heads of the thronging beasts, but this was no missed shot. The arrow flew forth, drawing an arc over Inglis's head.

"Burst!" At Rafinha's command, the arrow transformed from a single heavy shaft to a rain of flechettes falling down on the battlefield. This was the Shiny Flow.

The rain cut mercilessly through the mob of beasts, and as their death rattles arose, Inglis stepped nimbly out of the way. It was a difficult tactic to pull off, but that was exactly why Inglis liked it. These sorts of maneuvers had earned her a reputation. No one else on the battlefield would be able to dodge such an attack; it was the perfect way to bring about Rafinha's full power. They'd developed this while fighting side by side, using both of their strengths.

And as the arrows of light tapered off, only Inglis remained on her feet, brushing back her hair as she smiled and walked back to Rafinha. "Good job, Rani. You got 'em all. I'm impressed."

"They weren't that strong. You're the one who was amazing, charging in like that with no hesitation. I still don't understand how you can dodge Shiny Flow."

As the duo walked back toward the knights, they were met with a wave of shouted acclamation.

◆ ◇ ◆

That night, Inglis and Rafinha relaxed in a bath in the manor.

"This feels great! The lord here sure is generous, letting us unwind here! ♪"

The bath was large and made of stone, decorated with carvings. The water was on the warm side, but that just helped wash their exhaustion away. Rafinha hummed happily.

This had once been the lord's private bath, but the current lord allowed all to use it. That courtesy extended to even the new arrivals, Inglis and Rafinha, who had the bath to themselves, probably because it was so late.

"Agreed. It's been too long since we've been able to take a nice relaxing bath like this," Inglis said.

"All the food we can eat, and a fancy private room since we're girls. This is way better than some inn."

"They seem to have quite a high opinion of us. Guess all that hard work paid off."

The manor was already abuzz with tales of how the two of them had taken on dozens of magicite beasts and won. And their exploits had earned them a sizable bonus. The lord, the Highlander woman, had been too busy to meet with them today, but they were told she would receive them tomorrow.

"We blew 'em away! The Decoy Kaboom strategy wins again!" Rafinha cheered.

"I wish we had a better name for it..."

"Hey, you have to admit it's accurate. ♪" Rafinha stood. "C'mon. I'll get your back for you." She pointed to the spacious area for washing up.

## Chapter VII: Inglis, Age 15—The City Ruled by Highlanders (Part 1)

"Sure, but," Inglis paused, "maybe we can get towels first?"

Rafinha had one, but it was perched firmly on her head, and everywhere else was as unabashedly bare as the day she'd been born.

*She's definitely growing up,* Inglis thought. *A bit slender, but still.*

Water flowed down Rafinha's silky skin.

As Inglis stared, a feeling of guilt overtook her. *And that's why I'd rather we were wearing something.* Inglis swiftly draped her own towel over her body as she rose from the bath.

"Oh, c'mon, Chris. You don't need to get so embarrassed. What do we have to hide from each other?"

"Don't pull at my towel like that!"

"You've got a lot to show off! It'd be a shame to keep it hidden! Don't be shy, ha ha ha."

"Ugh, I thought you were just going to wash my back!"

"That was the plan, but you're so beautiful. I want to take this in for a moment. That voluptuous chest, those beautiful lines, that nice toned butt."

"Th-The more you say that, the more embarrassing it is."

To be perfectly honest, Rafinha was right. Inglis's body had changed a lot for a fifteen-year-old girl. She was acquiring the bearing of a grown woman. However, as good as she looked, she was uncomfortable with her chest. Sure, being well-endowed let her look good in some stunning outfits. She took that into account when choosing her clothes. It wasn't all bad. She still had reservations, though.

"I wish I looked like you," Rafinha said with a pause. "I'm so scrawny. Anyway, sit down. I'll get your back."

Inglis took a seat. "Don't worry about it. You're still growing, right? You'll do more than just get taller."

"I've been massaging them as much as I can. Isn't that supposed to make them bigger?" Rafinha lifted a sudsy towel and began to scrub Inglis's back.

"I know you've been trying."

"Chris, did you have to massage yours?"

"Nope."

"No fair! I'm so jealous!" Rafinha's eyes took on a strange gleam, unbeknownst to Inglis. "Gotcha!" Suddenly thrusting her arms under Inglis's, she latched onto her friend's chest.

"Eek?! R-Rani, what are you doing?!"

"Whoa! They're so big and jiggly! So that's what they feel like. Amazing! Mine are so different. You're lucky."

"Okay, okay, fine, you know now! So let go!"

"Hmmm. Not yet. ♪"

"Ugh! Enough! I'll wash your back now!"

As they bickered together, a woman entered the baths and called out to them. "Oh, is someone already here? You two certainly seem to be enjoying yourselves."

Her wavy, flaxen hair and soft eyes matched her graceful personality. On her forehead was a Rune-like mark—likely her stigmata. Surprisingly, she seemed to be in her late teens, only a little older than Inglis and Rafinha.

"Good evening," she said. "Are you the two young lady mercenaries I've heard so much about?"

"G-Good evening..." both girls said.

"I'm sorry I was unable to receive you properly. I'm Cyrene, consul to Nova." The Highlander smiled as she gave a small curtsy.

Inglis and Rafinha couldn't contain their nerves.

"My name is Inglis Eucus. I apologize for the noise just now."

"I'm Rafinha Bilford! Sorry for being so loud!"

"Oh, don't worry about it. There are plenty of louder bathers among us." Cyrene waved her hand casually, as if being a consul—and a Highlander, no less—meant nothing.

This unsettled Rafinha even more. "What do we do, Chris? She seems normal, but..." she whispered.

"I guess we just got lucky."

The waitress at lunch had thought she was a good person, and so

## Chapter VII: Inglis, Age 15—The City Ruled by Highlanders (Part 1)

did the people of the manor. She certainly seemed all right at first glance, but what could be hiding behind that smile?

"Sorry, I didn't catch that."

"Oh, nothing!" Inglis and Rafinha answered in unison.

"Mind if I join you for a chat? It seems like such a wonderful opportunity."

As Cyrene spoke, Inglis and Rafinha could hear the soft patter of footsteps coming from the hallway outside.

"Lady Cyrene!"

"Is it bath time?"

"We stayed up for this!"

A trio of young girls, four to six years old, ran into the room still fully-clothed.

*Adorable*, Inglis thought. *They remind me of Rafinha and me at that age.*

Cyrene called them by name. "Oh, my. Rino, Miyumi, Chico. You're still awake?"

A stout woman in her forties followed hot on their heels. "Oh no! You're getting your pajamas wet! Come on, back to bed with you..."

"It's fine, Mimosa. All right, everyone, get out of your pajamas! It's bath time! Just don't make any more trouble for Mimosa after this, okay?"

The children jumped for joy.

"Yay!"

"Race you!"

"I'm gonna be first!"

Their footsteps echoed down the hallway as they ran to change.

"Phew, they don't listen to a thing I say." Mimosa sighed.

"Sorry, Mimosa. I know it's hard work."

"No, I don't mind. I used to have a son, and he's... He's gone now, but they remind me of him." She smiled before following the children to help them change.

"See? It gets quite lively in here sometimes. And you haven't even heard the men yet." Cyrene smiled warmly.

As the children returned, the lively conversation in the bath turned to Inglis and Rafinha themselves, topics like Inglis's birth in the fortress city of Ymir, Rafinha's status as the duke's daughter, Inglis being the captain of the knight's daughter, their journey to the capital and the knights' academy there, their dwindling funds, and their choice to earn some coin by working with the knights.

"Aha ha ha! What a wonderful story! And all because of your bottomless stomachs."

"You have to admit, the food here is amazing. Right, Chris?"

"Yeah. It really is."

"Then that's yet another reason for me to be grateful for it," Cyrene said. "Without it, I'd never have met two amazing women like you."

Rafinha smiled. "We'll try our hardest not to be a burden!"

"We won't be here long, but we appreciate your generosity," Inglis said.

"And I must thank you as well." A calm, gentle expression rose to Cyrene's face.

Rafinha cut in. "Um, can I ask you something?"

"What is it?"

"Those children... Are they the ones we'd heard were being taken care of at the manor?"

"Yes. They'd lost their families and had to resort to begging in the alleys. I couldn't ignore that."

"Even though you're a Highlander?" Inglis probed.

"Maybe because I'm a Highlander."

"What do you mean?"

"In Highland, children don't suffer and starve like that. We have enough food from the surface that it's given out to whoever hungers."

"Huh. Interesting."

"It wasn't until my first visit to the surface, before I became the consul for Nova, that I saw children suffering like that. I realized my assumptions about how the world worked were just assumptions. I started thinking about what I could do to help. That's why I volunteered to become a consul. In this role, I can help children get off the streets, as well as people who are ill or disabled."

"I don't suppose there are many Highlanders who think like you," Inglis commented.

"You're not wrong. But it's not important what other Highlanders think—I only care about what I think, and I want to see these people smile." Cyrene's calm expression took on a firm intensity.

"Why, that's wonderful! I totally agree! We'll try our hardest! Just tell us what you need done!" Rafinha's eyes gleamed as she grasped Cyrene's hand. Her own strong sense of right and wrong gave her an instinctive feel for when others had similar convictions. She was also someone who judged people individually, not as a group. She fully supported Cyrene's motivations.

*Pure and innocent,* Inglis thought. *That's not necessarily a bad thing, but if Cyrene had been dispatched to Ymir, would Rafinha feel the same way?*

Maybe Rafinha would have. Cyrene definitely seemed to be honest about her motivations. She wasn't the one who decided to cede land to Highland; she was simply the one who was sent to run it. It was possible her higher-ups did not share her views, though.

"Why, thank you!" Cyrene's smile gleamed. Maybe she and Rafinha were on the same wavelength.

"There's one thing I'd like to ask..." Inglis spoke up.

"Yes, go ahead."

"The flow of mana seems strange here. Is there some reason for that?"

Ever since Inglis had arrived in Nova, she'd felt an eerie pull, like something was dragging the mana of the residents down. Or maybe sucking it away from them? But since almost no one on the surface understood mana, they couldn't tell. Plus, the force wasn't strong enough to affect their health. Inglis had noticed Rafinha was moving slower ever

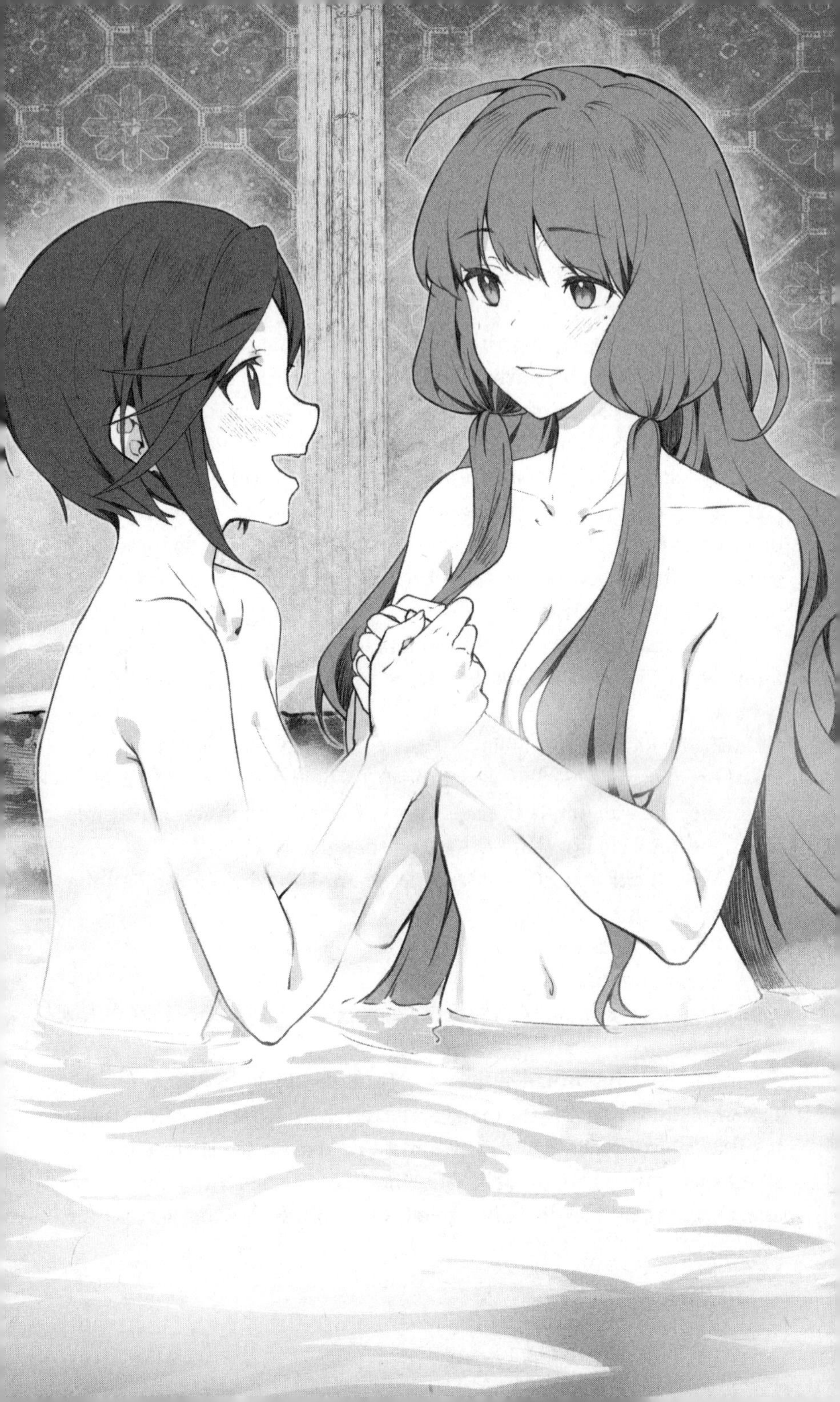

## Chapter VII: Inglis, Age 15—The City Ruled by Highlanders (Part 1)

since their arrival in Nova, and that was one reason why she had wanted to leave quickly. Although, now that they were here, she had to know what was going on. There could be a worthy foe nearby.

*If there is, I'd like to fight it. Was I really only twelve when I last had a satisfying fight? There's been nothing since Eris, Leon, and Rahl. A three-year drought. C'mon, I don't want to wait all my life.*

Cyrene shook her head. "I'm sorry. I don't know."

"I see…"

"I'm not really sure what you mean," Rafinha said, "but are you sure you're not imagining things, Chris?"

"Hmm, that's possible." *Guess I'll check it out myself, then.*

"Can I ask you two a few things, too?" Cyrene inquired.

"Of course!" Rafinha immediately promised.

"Sure, ask away," Inglis added.

Cyrene's eyes were deadly serious. "Well, could I ask for your help with something that's not a magicite beast problem but rather a people problem?"

◆◇◆

Cyrene laid out the situation to Inglis and Rafinha: The previous lord's knights were making their move. Having maintained their command structure after their dismissal, they had orchestrated several attacks on patrols in the city. Cyrene thought even open rebellion was a possible next step. She had hoped to nip the situation in the bud with rumors of a punitive expedition, but the rebels had reacted by drawing together all their forces for an ambush.

That left the option of a single pitched battle. The rebels outnumbered and outmatched the current knights, but the presence of prodigies like Inglis could change the outcome of the fight. And because Inglis and Rafinha had limited time in Nova, Cyrene decided now was the time to strike.

An urgent plea to save Nova—Inglis was honestly a bit surprised that Cyrene would propose such a risky plan upon first meeting a new mercenary, despite their similar ages and Inglis's obvious skills. Was it rashness? Was it valor? Or was Cyrene's back simply to the wall? Inglis had no way to tell, but Rafinha's enthusiasm suggested that Cyrene did at least have an eye for finding allies. Perhaps the trustworthiness they both shared had brought the three together.

As long as Rafinha wanted to help, Inglis didn't have any personal objections. Of course, she didn't have any ideological enthusiasm for the cause. Inglis Eucus had sworn to avoid all of that. This was just a desire to protect Rafinha and find a worthy foe. She doubted she'd find someone like that among the riff-raff of local mercenaries, though.

Three nights after Cyrene had made her request, Inglis marched forth as part of a strike force making their way to an abandoned church outside the city. There were about thirty knights in all, led personally by Cyrene, who expected the rebels would come with greater numbers, only to be defeated and captured. Cyrene had ordered that none be killed if at all possible. If nothing else, Inglis found that to be a more appealing challenge than simply slaughtering them. It was likely one that appealed greatly to Rafinha, too.

"We can see the church now, Chris," Rafinha murmured.

"Yeah. It's about time for the ambushers to show up."

There was plenty of dense cover around the ruined church, including a cave. With all the places to hide, it was the perfect site for an ambush. Inglis could sense them waiting.

"Here they come. Cyrene, everyone, be careful," Inglis warned.

Cyrene solemnly nodded. "Of course! I believe in you."

"Don't worry," Nash, now with the group again, said. "We'll protect you with our lives!" He was fired up and ready for battle, hoping his cheer would be infectious for Cyrene's benefit.

As Cyrene's knights advanced, the enemy streamed forth from the church, the cave, and the surrounding forest.

"Whoa! Here they come! Just like you thought, Chris!"

## Chapter VII: Inglis, Age 15—The City Ruled by Highlanders (Part 1)

"Looks that way." Inglis calmly counted the opposing force. There were nearly a hundred foes, three times what Cyrene had been able to muster.

In other words, they would pose no real problem.

A burly middle-aged man emerged from the church, crowing in triumph. "Ha ha ha ha! We saw right through your plan! And now we've got our Highland usurper right here to get her just deserts!"

"That's Hawker, the old knight captain! He's their leader!" Nash explained to Inglis.

Rafinha took up a position in the lead. "So we just have to capture him, right? Let's go!" She began to charge a weak Shiny Flow, not strong enough to kill anyone but enough to knock them down. Being able to control the power behind an attack was an advantage of her Artifact.

Hawker taunted Cyrene's force. "Ha ha! You're outnumbered! There's no way you can stand against us!"

"It's not how many troops you have—it's how you use them!" Rafinha yelled. "More of you just gives me more targets!" Rafinha let loose her shot, and—"Burst!" The arrow of light split and rained down on the rebels.

"Whoa?!" people screamed.

Ten or so rebels were smashed flat, much to their surprise.

"What?! An upper-class rune and Artifact?!"

She might not have been quite the all-powerful savior that holy knights were seen as, but to the average soldier, she was still plenty awe-inspiring.

"Sorry, this is probably overkill for you guys!" Rafinha began to charge a second shot.

"Hold it right there." A spear flew through the sky and smashed the arrow with a deafening crash.

"Huh? What?!" Rafinha gasped.

The thrower of the spear was a woman with vivid, flowing red hair, who looked around twenty years old. She was tall and slender, beautiful, but the most striking thing about her was her clear, intent gaze.

"Sorry, but I'm gonna have to take you out. You got unlucky running into me." She effortlessly pulled her spear from the ground as she spoke.

"Ahhh! Watching Sistia fight gives me the chills!" a rebel said.

"Quiet down," Sistia ordered as she paced toward Rafinha single-mindedly. "I'll handle her. You guys take out the cannon fodder."

Inglis recognized her bearing, her aura. This was a hieral menace! She'd felt this same thing from Eris. Why Sistia was here didn't matter—all that mattered was that a hieral menace was right here, leading the enemy. That was enough to make the situation worthwhile to Inglis.

*What luck! The first chance in three years to see how far I've come!* Inglis thought. She tried her hardest not to show her enthusiasm as she stepped between Rafinha and Sistia.

"Rani, protect Cyrene and the others. I'll take her on."

"Okay," Rafinha said, hesitating. "You know, Chris, you always seem really happy at times like this."

"Huh? You noticed?" To Inglis, it was embarrassing to look too hungry for a fight, so she had actually been trying to hide her glee.

"Of course. Your eyes look completely different, and you keep smiling for no reason."

"R-Really?"

*So she knew the whole time?* Inglis thought. *Dammit, she probably thinks I've been messing with her.*

"And what do we have here? A powerless little girl looking for a fight? Is this some kind of bad joke?" Sistia mocked.

"Heh heh heh." A charming, innocent smile drew across Inglis's face as she converted the aether wrapped around her into mana. As soon as she did, Sistia's expression changed.

"Wh-What?! But I didn't sense anything until—"

It was vital for Inglis to show opponents her strength in a way they'd understand, so they wouldn't hold back. She was grateful she'd taught herself that technique.

"I can't believe it," Cyrene said, drawing in her breath. "Inglis is incredible..."

## Chapter VII: Inglis, Age 15—The City Ruled by Highlanders (Part 1)

Even though Cyrene had taken notice, too, neither Inglis nor Sistia paid her any attention as they squared off.

"Don't think you're the strongest one here just because you're a hieral menace. There are powers beyond even your ken." Inglis's eyes glimmered with the sharpness and intensity of a warrior's. "No holding back. No showing off. Just bring everything you've got." She smiled as she tensed for battle.

"Very well. I haven't had a good fight in a while. Maybe this will stave off my boredom momentarily. I'll take you on." Sistia swept her spear's head through the air before grinning and taking up her fighting stance.

Not all hieral menaces were as reticent to fight as Eris. Sistia may have been shocked for a moment by the enormous amount of mana Inglis could manifest, but it wasn't enough to cow her.

*Now this is my kind of opponent.*

"Looks like we're on the same page. I've been feeling the same way for three years now."

Inglis felt truly lucky to have met Eris. When she met her again, they'd be on the same side. They might have the opportunity to spar, but it would never be a real fight.

"You're a cheeky little brat, poking your nose where it doesn't belong. I'm gonna have to smash it so flat, you won't be able to poke it anywhere else." Sistia readied the golden point of her spear as the tip gleamed.

*That's the bloodthirstiness I'm looking for! Enough to make my hair stand on end! I've been waiting for someone like this!*

"Draw your sword, then," Sistia challenged, waiting for Inglis.

All Inglis had was a normal sword. When she had fought with Eris, a similar blade had broken. The same was likely to happen in this battle. When it did break, it would be a moment of vulnerability for Inglis, so it would be better not to draw it to begin with. Even though Inglis had a sword on her, that didn't mean she had much use for it. It couldn't do anything to magicite beasts, and it'd be destroyed by any serious amount of aether, so Inglis couldn't combine it with Aether Shell. Artifacts would do the same—at least, the lowest class of Artifacts. She hadn't tried fighting against anything better with a plain sword, because it'd be a waste if it broke in combat.

The inability of ordinary weapons to stand up to aether had irked Inglis even in her previous life. As a king, she'd overcome it with a holy sword, but Inglis Eucus was not yet worthy of such a weapon. Even if she wanted one, she might as well have asked for the moon.

"Why bother? It's just a chunk of metal. Now, come on! Show me what you've got!" Inglis said.

"Hmph. Let's find out if you can back your talk up!"

Sistia suddenly leaped forward with the intensity of a gale. In the blink of an eye, she closed the gap between the two, thrusting her spear at Inglis's face. A normal knight would have been taken down before they could so much as step out of the way, but Inglis tilted her head, letting the point whistle by her ear. The best dodge used the smallest of movements.

Not that such a thing took Sistia by surprise. "Mm-hm!"

It was merely a test. If Inglis couldn't easily avoid that attack, then she wouldn't be worthy as an opponent.

"How about this?!"

The next attack was an even faster, fiercer triple strike, swift enough for lesser opponents to think the spear had split into three, but it still wasn't Sistia's full potential. Just as before, Inglis twisted out of the way with the minimum effort possible, not even falling back but instead advancing a step with every dodge.

"Hmph, not bad!"

Sistia used more speed, more power, but the thrusts cut around Inglis as the younger girl continued her advance.

"Tch!"

The closer Inglis got, the harder it was for Sistia to effectively use her spear. A step back, another series of thrusts—her attacks all had the same result. Each time Sistia pulled her spear back to thrust again, Inglis advanced. It was proof Inglis had full confidence in her evasion. Sistia, a master of the weapon, saw that proof firsthand.

## Chapter VII: Inglis, Age 15—The City Ruled by Highlanders (Part 1)

*I'm being driven back?!* she thought. *And by someone who's not even attacking—just dodging?!*

"Gah!" Sistia felt her back collide with something hard. It was the wall of the church. She hadn't realized she'd been pushed back so far. Inglis was eating up all her focus.

But if there was no more falling back...

"Haaah!" Sistia let loose a series of thrusts with all her might. This was an attack she was proud of, one capable of smashing giant boulders.

Somehow, not a single strike found its mark.

The smack of a hand falling on her shoulder broke her out of her battle reverie.

"Wow, that was pretty good."

"Wh—?!" Sistia exclaimed, looking up at an angelic grin in front of her face.

Its innocent cuteness scared her more than anything. Shivers ran up and down her spine. Suddenly, something smashed into her belly—Inglis's fist. Sistia's body doubled over before flying backward through the wall of the church. She tumbled along its floor before coming to a stop.

"Ugh..." Swaying a little, she stumbled to her feet. Hieral menaces were, in a word, tough. They could endure far more pain than the average human. About as much as a holy knight, even. They were just built differently.

*I'm not done yet!* Sistia's eyes still gleamed with fighting passion.

Inglis spoke quietly to herself as she followed Sistia inside. "Yeah. I'm getting..." She trailed off as her mind began to race.

She was just able to take on a hieral menace without a weapon, and then deliver an attack of her own. Three years ago, even with a weapon, she was pinned down. This time, she was able to go on the offensive. She was definitely getting better.

She nodded approvingly at her own self-improvement. All that practice with Rafinha's Shiny Flow had taught her a lot about evasion. Lately, seeing the arrows coming had become boring, though, so she had started dodging with her eyes closed and her ears blocked.

"Damn you!" Sistia glared at Inglis with the energy of a mad dog.

"You've still got tricks left, right? Show me. Even Eris had an ace up her sleeve. I want to see what yours is."

"Eris... That must be one of this kingdom's hieral menaces."

"You know her?"

"I know *of* her. We've never met in person."

Eris was one of only two hieral menaces in this country, meaning she was famous in her own right. It wasn't surprising that Sistia would have heard of her.

*And then the other's...Ripple, I think? Definitely not Sistia, though.*

"Can I ask you one thing? Just who are you? What's an extra hieral menace doing here?" Inglis peppered her with questions.

"Hmph. None of your business."

No real answer. Not that Inglis really cared, and she wasn't curious enough to make her answer.

"And what about you?" Sistia asked.

Inglis looked at her quizzically.

"You have so much power. Why are you using it in a Highlander's service? Don't you realize they're trying to take the surface for themselves? Are you just going to watch it happen? Or worse, help them?"

Inglis thought over her words carefully. "Cyrene seems kind. Everyone in the manor likes her."

Only three days in Cyrene's service had shown Inglis how highly Cyrene's retinue regarded the woman. She was extremely popular with the locals, especially the orphans who treated her like a surrogate mother.

"I don't think it matters *who* rules in comparison to *how* they rule," Inglis insisted.

"Maybe if you only want to see the obvious. By the time you realize what's really going on, it'll be too late. Haven't you noticed what's happening in this city?"

"You mean, how the mana flows? What of it?"

## Chapter VII: Inglis, Age 15—The City Ruled by Highlanders (Part 1)

"Better you find out for yourself."

*So maybe there is something going on there, but...*

"...I'm not completely unconcerned, but I'm not here to fight for a cause," Inglis retorted.

"What?"

"I simply ate more than I budgeted for, so I'm helping her out to earn some money. But now I'm grateful for my appetite. If not for that, we'd never have been able to fight like this."

"You're happy so long as you're fighting? What's the value in power without purpose?"

"Having fun. That's it."

"You fool!" Sistia screamed, enraged at such an answer. "Without purpose, you may as well be a machine!"

"That's not true. Power is a record of your experiences, your gifts, your practice, and your past battles. It's fighting without any of those, just an ideal, that makes you a machine." Inglis reflected on her past life, spent so devoted to her country and its people that she'd had no time for herself. Even just fifteen years of experience may well have brought her further than that lifetime ever did.

"Shut up! People like you don't deserve to have power!"

"Then take me down and prove it. If you still think you can." Inglis smirked.

"Silence! You're just making fun of me!" It was an obvious provocation, but one a proud woman like Sistia couldn't ignore. She turned a wrathful gaze toward Inglis.

With a low rumble, the very air around Sistia twisted, like she was a mirage.

"Can you handle this?!" She thrust her spear from too far away to reach Inglis, but somehow its point seemed to bend around.

*Behind me!* Inglis twisted away reflexively, but the golden spearpoint followed, skimming along her side. It was a light wound, but it was still enough to cut through her clothing and draw blood.

"Hmph. Good reflexes."

"Not bad! I knew you had it in you!" Inglis cheered.

A thrust from outside range that suddenly twisted around and struck from behind—so Sistia could bend space for her attacks.

*So this is what a hieral menace is really capable of. She's dangerous. I avoided that one on reflex, but if she keeps it up...then that's exactly what I'm looking for! A worthy opponent!*

"It's my turn to laugh now!" Sistia raised her spear again.

"Hah!" Inglis immediately ran as fast as she could. The spear pieced the floor at her feet, but she kept dashing through the church. At full speed, even if Sistia's thrust came from behind or tried to pin her down, Inglis could avoid it. Coming to a stop was far more dangerous.

"Haaaah!"

*Rumble, rumble, rumble!*

Sistia's spear pierced holes in the floor, the windows, the walls, everywhere until the church was riddled with gaps. However, at Inglis's speed, a few scrapes aside, not one of the blows landed true.

"How about this?!" Suddenly, the tip of the spear appeared dead-center in Inglis's vision.

Inglis had been avoiding Sistia's attacks by always sprinting out of the way when they arrived, but this was one attack she couldn't outpace. That wasn't a problem, though. It was what she had been waiting for!

"There it is!" Inglis reached out her hand and grabbed the tip of the spear. *If I'm ready... I can do this!*

"Ngh! What are you—?!" Sistia tried to pull her spear back, but Inglis's grip was firm.

"Now what?" Inglis locked eyes with Sistia—and got a smug grin back.

"You fool! Now I've stopped you!"

Inglis saw Sistia's long, lithe leg swing into the air and felt something crash into her abdomen. Sistia's leg had somehow stretched over the distance and struck Inglis.

## Chapter VII: Inglis, Age 15—The City Ruled by Highlanders (Part 1)

*So her kicks can do the same thing as her spear! That's a surprise.*

That meant if Inglis caught the spear, she was still in danger. Sistia had tricked her. Hieral menaces were really talented. Even when Inglis thought she got under Sistia's skin, it didn't stop the hieral menace from looking for openings!

"Ugh...?!" The kick had sent Inglis flying into the air, where she was absolutely vulnerable.

*There's no way I can react in time!* she panicked.

"Got you!" Sistia immediately thrust her spear to tear through Inglis.

*Then take this!*

"Haaaaaaaaah!" A ball of cold light wrapped around Inglis's body.

She had activated Aether Shell. Sistia's spear struck her from behind just as the shell blinked into existence, rendering the attack fruitless. The tip barely grazed Inglis's skin before it was repelled by the aether.

"What?!" The cold light of the aether condensed into a wave, shielding Inglis from harm. All the might behind Sistia's thrust couldn't penetrate it.

Sistia gasped in surprise. "Impossible!"

Her priority had come down to what she could do before Inglis recovered. That was her chance, and even repelled at first, she did not give up. In the end, none of her blows struck true, and Inglis was regaining her footing. Upon landing, the girl had crouched, shoved off the floor—

And disappeared.

At least, that was how it looked to Sistia. It was as if a single bolt of lightning had struck.

*Crashhh!*

Suddenly, Sistia felt herself being lifted into the air as a shock like she'd never felt before struck her solar plexus. She had never noticed the knee whirling toward her. "Agh! Ugh... I can't believe..."

Her knees hit the ground, her legs trembling and unable to lift her back up. Her spear, slipping from her hands, clattered to the floor.

Again, Inglis clapped her on her shoulder, smiling in approval. "That was a good fight. It was a lot more fun than I expected."

Inglis had simply countered with a knee after shielding herself with Aether Shell. Because that technique boosted her physical capabilities tremendously, Sistia simply couldn't perceive Inglis at full speed.

*I still couldn't pull it off without using aether, though,* Inglis lamented silently. *There's a lot I need to keep working on. Thanks for showing me that.*

"Gah! I'll never be able to face—"

Just then, a third voice cut in. "Chris! We've captured everyone outside! How are you— Gccck?! Ngh!" Rafinha had come to check on Inglis but immediately found a hand wrapped around her own neck.

"Rani?!"

"Don't move!" Sistia commanded. She had closed the distance in the blink of an eye to put Rafinha in a choke hold.

Inglis stayed quiet, still.

"I can't let myself be captured here! If you want her to live, let me go!" Sistia said desperately.

"Sure, fine. You're leaving? Go right ahead." Inglis held up her hands to make it clear that she wasn't going to stop Sistia.

Sistia circled warily around Inglis, not averting her eyes even as she picked up her spear and made her way to the back door of the church. Her staggered gait made her injuries clear.

"I have one other thing to say to you," Inglis said.

"What?"

"If you want to fight me, I'm ready anytime. If you think it's not going well, go ahead—back off and regroup. I want the practice. I want to get stronger. I'll fight you as many times as you like. But if you ever lay a finger on Rani again, you're a dead woman."

Sistia didn't know what to say to that.

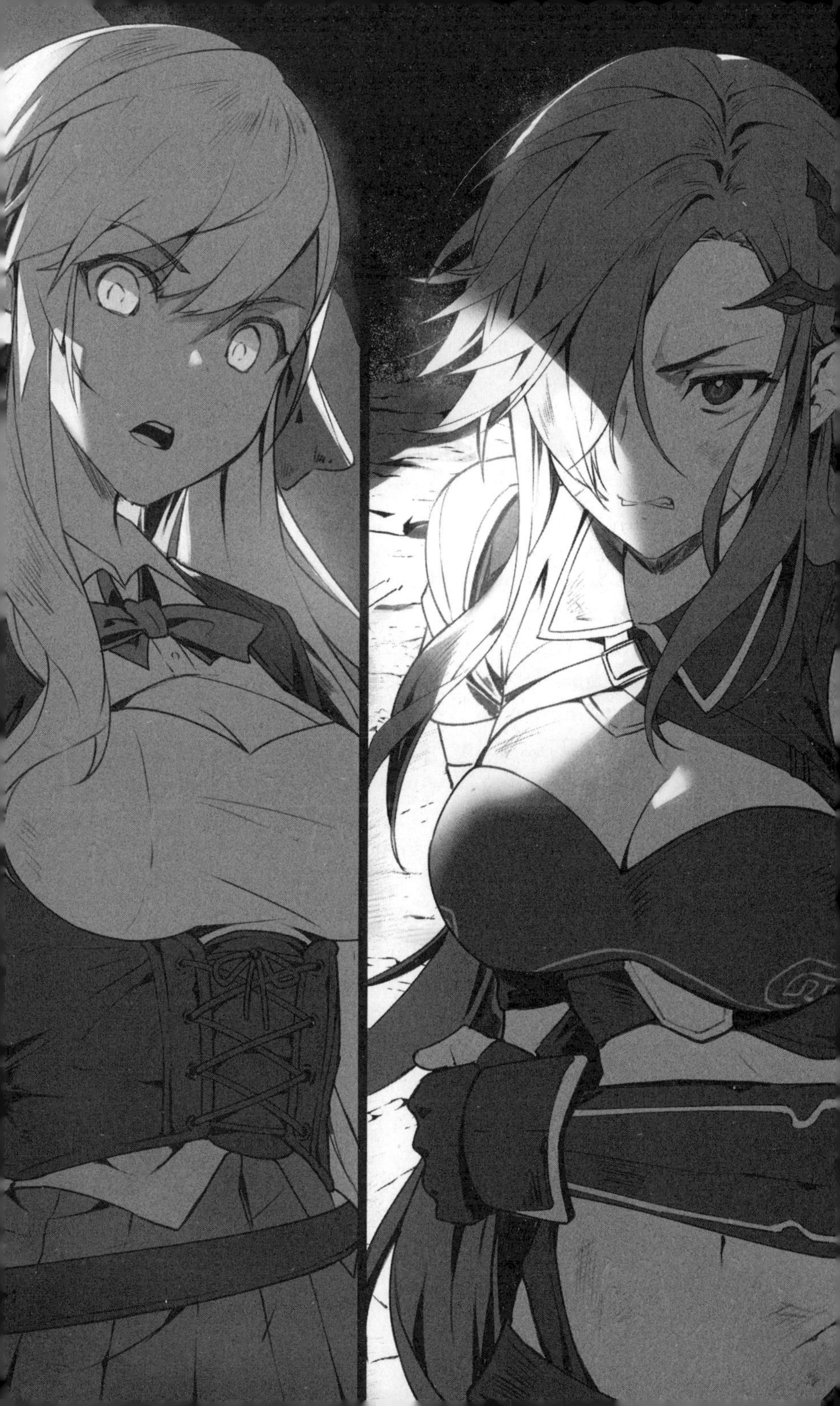

For a moment, a cold, murderous look swept across Inglis's face. Sistia shivered in horror. It was far worse than any she'd seen even during the fight.

At that moment, Sistia fully understood the depths of Inglis's passion.

"That's all. Until we meet again." As suddenly as it had appeared, Inglis's sharp gaze softened, replaced with the innocent smile of a girl who wouldn't hurt a fly.

Sistia couldn't understand her at all. Who on earth was this girl?

Before Sistia realized words were coming out of her mouth, she asked, "What's your name?"

"Inglis Eucus."

"I'm Sistia Rouge. Until we meet again." Sistia let loose her grip on Rafinha and slipped away.

"Rani! Are you okay?!"

Rafinha coughed for a bit before speaking. "Yeah, I'm fine. Sorry to ruin the moment like that."

"Don't worry about it. The fight was already over, so it's fine. Let's head back if you're done, too." Inglis pulled Rafinha to her feet and patted her head.

"Yeah, we got 'em all. There should be a nice big reward waiting for us."

"Yeah. I'm satisfied with how my end turned out, too. I haven't had a fun fight like that in a while. Sometimes your ideas turn out really well."

"All right, let's head back."

"Yeah."

Inglis and Rani smiled as they nodded to each other.

# Chapter VIII: Inglis, Age 15—The City Ruled by Highlanders (Part 2)

The next day, the townspeople came to the square to watch the presentation of the captured rebels.

What awaited these former knights? An execution, presumably. What other fate could await the attempted assassins of Nova's lord?

"Well, we were the ones who caught them. It's our responsibility to see the whole process through," Rafinha said to herself—even though she really didn't want to watch.

Cyrene stood before the former knights in judgment, expressionless through their jeers and curses. "It is I who drove you out, so I understand your resentment, but I want you to understand you chose the wrong path. Might gives you no right to look down on the weak. People should be respected as people. They should be treated as equals. I wish I could have taught you that."

The townspeople, who had long suffered under those knights during the previous lord's reign, rose in applause. Some of the rebels stared at the ground in repentance, some cursed Cyrene's name. She watched them silently for a moment before delivering an order to her own retinue.

"Free them."

"What?" Nash exclaimed after a pause, confused. "Cyrene, you're letting them live?!"

Cyrene nodded to him before kneeling in front of the ex-captain, Hawker. "I'm asking you to turn over a new leaf and join us. In a world with the threat of magicite beasts, people must join hand in hand, not fight among themselves! Please! Use your power not for yourself, but for the powerless!" She bowed so deeply that her stigmata, the symbol of Highland's pride, scraped along the ground.

Her humility amazed the crowd. Most Highlanders arrogantly looked down on surface-dwellers as subhuman, but Cyrene... Cyrene definitely seemed to be something else entirely.

Inglis watched as the townspeople's loyalty began to spread even to the ex-knights.

"She's forgiving us...?" a rebel said.

"No. I'm the one asking for your forgiveness for what I've done to you. If you can't bring yourself to forgive me, you may leave. Just please... please don't repeat the same cycle wherever you go."

It was Hawker's turn to kneel in front of her, completely overwhelmed. "Yes, ma'am! I owe you my life! Use it as you see fit!" Clearing his throat, he turned to his troops. "Listen up, men! We were full of ourselves, but that changes now!"

At his call, his comrades kneeled before Cyrene as the townspeople gave thunderous applause. Today was a new beginning for the town of Nova.

"Wow! Cyrene, you're so cool! Right, Chris?" Rafinha exclaimed, just as overjoyed as the townspeople were.

"Ha ha ha. She sure is."

Quite the opposite of being executed, the old knights had been reinstated, which would greatly increase Nova's ability to defend itself. It was quite the clever plan.

*Bold, perhaps too bold. But a sure sign of Cyrene's youthful enthusiasm. In my past life, I'd have had an eye on her as a potential minister,* Inglis thought.

## Chapter VIII: Inglis, Age 15—The City Ruled by Highlanders (Part 2)

"I thank you all!" Cyrene's heartfelt delight brought smiles to those around her.

That night, there was a celebratory banquet at the manor. Inglis and Rafinha were able to enjoy the delicacies of Nova to their hearts' content—not to mention to the shock of their comrades-in-arms.

When they were fully satisfied, Cyrene came to talk. Leaving the banquet early for the privacy of the lord's suite, they spoke over tea.

"That turned out so well, Cyrene! You're amazing!" Rafinha said with a small gasp of awe.

Cyrene chuckled. "Really, I was so scared my legs were shaking. I'm exhausted." She stifled a yawn, and gave a cute, yet apologetic, smile.

"Why, that won't do at all. I've added an herb which will ease away your worries to tonight's tea. Drink and relax." The woman who looked after Cyrene and the orphans—Mimosa, her name was—smiled as she appeared with a freshly-brewed pot.

"Thank you, Mimosa. Hmm, this tastes a bit different. Not bad at all, though. I already feel refreshed. It really does carry the exhaustion away."

Rafinha and Inglis took a sip from their own cups.

"It's delicious."

"Yeah, thank you."

The trio chatted casually for a short while, before Cyrene changed the topic. "There's something important I want to show you two. Follow me." Her warm expression from before was gone.

"Oh? Show us what?" Inglis asked.

"What's this about?" Rafinha tilted her head.

Cyrene only hinted at the subject, her words trailing off. "It's about what you mentioned before."

*The flow of mana here, I guess?*

"Please lead the way, then." Now that Inglis's finances were in a good spot, she had been conflicted between investigating it and moving on to their next destination. With Cyrene being the one to approach them, she could use this as an opportunity.

Cyrene took Inglis and Rafinha from her suite to a secret passage running underneath the castle. It was so well-hidden that only Cyrene knew about it—but there was still a magical barrier preventing the passage of any but a Highlander. Cyrene dispelled it for a moment and led Inglis and Rafinha further inside.

After much walking, they arrived at the deepest point of the passage, which opened to a vast, empty hall, its cobblestone floor taken up almost entirely by a vast magic circle marked with strange, eldritch patterns. It glowed faintly as Inglis sensed the mana being drawn down into it.

"What am I looking at? Is this magic circle gathering mana?" Inglis asked.

*This must be why mana flows so strangely in Nova—an underground circle, drawing mana from the inhabitants.*

"Wh-What *is* this, Cyrene?" Rafinha drew away slightly, creeped out by the strangeness of it all.

"This is the core of Highland—the Floating Circle. It draws mana from its surroundings, and when it's stored enough, the entire area detaches from the earth and floats into the sky. It becomes a new part of Highland." Cyrene pointed upward as she spoke.

Inglis took a breath in sharply. "So that's what..."

*So that's what Sistia, the hieral menace, meant when she said Highland was trying to take the surface for themselves.*

Inglis had thought she'd meant temporal power, or even religious power, but no. It was physically raising the land into the sky. In the most literal sense, Highland was taking the land for themselves.

"Whaaat?! So the entire town's going to fly away? Then what happens to the people who live here?!" Rafinha fretted. Inglis wanted to know the answer to that as well.

"A new Highland is for Highlanders," Cyrene explained. "So they'll be driven out, made into slaves, or in the worst case the city will be burned, according to what my superiors say."

"So everyone here is going to be exiled, enslaved, or killed?! No!" Rafinha protested.

## Chapter VIII: Inglis, Age 15—The City Ruled by Highlanders (Part 2)

"That's something I won't allow." Cyrene's expression became serious and determined, and she gazed up at the ceiling as if she could see through stone and fixate on Highland itself. "I don't care what they have planned. I came here to ease the suffering of those living on the surface. So I won't let anything bad happen to these people. I've insisted to them that any who want to rise with Nova be allowed to live freely, not as slaves. If they must become anything, they should be Highlanders themselves. That way, everyone will be able to live peacefully."

"Do you really think they'll go along with that?" Inglis asked.

The corners of Cyrene's mouth tightened. "If they don't, I'm willing to go to war."

"So that's why you forgave the rebels—to have them at your command if that came to pass."

Cyrene nodded. "Yes. I want to be able to defend this town, come what may."

"Cyrene." Inglis stared at her. "Why are you telling us this?"

"Maybe it's because I want forgiveness. No matter how much I improve things as the consul here, I also carry the seed of ruin with me. I know, yet I keep it a secret. And I haven't convinced myself that hiding it is the right choice. That's why I'm asking you. Do you think I'm doing the right thing?" Cyrene's smile was lonely as she looked at Inglis and Rafinha. "If you believe I'm wrong, strike me down. My death will awaken the guardian of the Floating Circle. But I believe you'll be able to defeat it while protecting the townspeople. Please, if it comes to that." Cyrene clenched the cuffs of her coat as she bowed her head.

The two could see her fingers shaking. "What do we do, Chris?" Rafinha asked nervously.

"Rani, your answer to Cyrene's question is the one that matters, not mine. You need to find your own path."

"But what about you, Chris? What do you think?"

"Me? My opinion is yours, of course. After all, I am your squire."

"What?! I have to decide all by myself? That's no fair!"

"That's what it means to lead, Rani. Get used to it."

Inglis had already lived a life of marking her beliefs on the world around her. Now it was time for a new generation to take up the mantle. And yet—Not a word of the Silvare Kingdom, built up according to King Inglis's ideals over an entire lifetime, appeared in the histories available in Ymir. Its king had left behind a utopia, only to reemerge in another era of suffering. Countries like Highland still sought to dominate their neighbors.

Her entire life's work from another time had faded from existence like the foam that crested a wave. Inglis couldn't deny she felt empty, realizing how little she accomplished. So if history really did repeat itself, then there was no point in getting herself involved again. All she could do was live her own life and try to squeeze as much joy out of it as possible.

"Yeah. I understand, Chris." Rafinha's expression turned determined, yet dignified, as she took a deep breath. She grasped Cyrene's hand. "Cyrene, I believe in you! I know you believe in the path you've chosen. Take good care of Nova and its people."

"Rafinha!" Cyrene beamed.

"If you need us when the town rises into the sky, we'll be there! We have to go to the knights' academy at the capital now, but that just means we'll be even better when the time comes! We'll be your knights!" Rafinha's smile was as bright as a blooming sunflower.

"Thank you! Thank you so much, Rafinha!" Cyrene latched her arms around Rafinha, tears in her eyes, and Rafinha returned the embrace.

*They really do get along well. Maybe Rafinha's found her match.* Inglis couldn't help but feel just a little bit jealous.

"Is it really right for me to decide this all by myself, Chris?"

"Yeah. It's fine. If all goes well, I'll get to take on Highland's army!"

"That doesn't sound like things going well at all!" Rafinha fired back.

◆ ◇ ◆

After Cyrene finished explaining herself, she retired to her room to rest while Inglis and Rafinha headed for the baths. They'd worked

## Chapter VIII: Inglis, Age 15—The City Ruled by Highlanders (Part 2)

hard—and been well rewarded for it—so the next day they'd be ready to set out again. But not before one last chance to enjoy a warm, relaxing bath.

"Ahh, this feels great. ♪ Too bad we have to say goodbye to these baths." Rafinha stretched out as she let the water wash over her.

"Until graduation, at least."

"Yep. I'm glad we ended up here, though. It really makes me feel like my time at the academy's going to pay off too. If nothing else, we'll be able to help Cyrene!"

"Definitely. We had a lot of fun, and there's lots to look forward to when we come back." Inglis couldn't hide her excitement at what awaited them.

"You really do have the soul of a warlord in the body of an angel... Shall I wash your back?"

Inglis stared at her.

"Huh, are you still on edge about that?"

"After that last time, of course! Don't grab my chest again, okay?"

Rafinha paused. "I promise I won't. This time it's your butt's turn."

"Absolutely not!"

Their playful bickering suddenly took a backseat to another noise.

*Rrrrrumble!*
*Grooooooan!*

The entire manor began to shake. Shouts from people inside echoed up to the baths as stone fell from the ceiling.

"Ah! Aaaaah! An earthquake?!"

"Seems like a pretty big one."

Inglis and Rafinha huddled together to wait it out, but as the shaking stopped, there were different cries.

"It— It's a magicite beast! There's magicite beasts!"

"To arms, to arms! Protect the consul!"

"Women and children, evacuate to the basement!"

The shouts of surprise were turning into screams of panic.

"A magicite beast?!" Inglis shouted. "With no warning from the watchtowers?" She could tell something was wrong.

"Time for us to lend a hand! We can't let anything happen to Cyrene," Rafinha said.

"Yeah. Let's hurry up and get dressed."

They both stood from the bath to hear a deafening sound.

*Boooom!*

The ceiling of the bath exploded. Fortunately, the mountain of rubble fell away from Inglis and Rafinha, leaving them unharmed. That wasn't all good news, though.

*Hisssss!*
*Squeeeak!*

A flood of low-slung magicite beasts with ratlike bodies leaped down through the hole in the ceiling. Each of the dozen or so beasts was as large as a lion or tiger, big enough to make a meal of a human.

Inglis turned to Rafinha. "Rani, I'll hold them off. Go get our clothes and your Artifact."

Fighting naked wasn't the most appealing idea in the world to Inglis, but there didn't seem to be much of an alternative.

"Got it, Chris."

"Here goes, then!" Inglis stepped forward to draw the beasts' attention. The nearest three formed up side-by-side and rushed at her.

"You sure have terrible manners, attacking a girl in the bath!"

Setting the pace, Inglis made the first move. She was on them in the blink of an eye, delivering a swift high kick to the lead beast's head that slammed it back into the wall before spinning around with the remaining momentum. Next was a backhand blow that sent the second beast following the same path as its leader. Finally, following through, she

### Chapter VIII: Inglis, Age 15—The City Ruled by Highlanders (Part 2)

swung her leg around into the last of the three. The force of her kick sent it slamming into the other two against the wall.

"I'm not done yet!" The first three were just the beginning, as Inglis knocked the beasts into a pile by the wall, buying time for Rafinha to get their things. Before long, all of them were slammed into one heap.

"Hmm. Not bad." An observer might have been amazed, but this was just a warmup for Inglis. Physical blows alone couldn't take down these creatures.

They'd be back up shortly.

She took a breath. "Here goes."

She didn't have the time to wait for Rafinha to come back and finish off the beasts. Inglis extended her index finger, and as the cold light of aether swirled around it, she pointed at the squirming beasts.

"Take this!"

*Pshhh!*

A thin beam of aether sprang forth from her index finger, piercing not just the beasts but the wall as it sailed into the night sky. The beasts shuddered to a halt.

This was Aether Pierce, a concentrated beam of aether. Aether attacks were powerful and affected a broad area, but they were hard to control precisely. By limiting both the power and area affected, she could reduce the effort necessary to control the attack. She felt drained even when using this technique, but it taking less effort was proof that her control of aether was improving. It was certainly something she'd never been able to accomplish in her past life; Inglis Eucus was making real progress. She'd been so happy the first time she'd pulled it off.

"I'm back, Chris!" Rafinha called, running in. "Wow, you already took them out! You're so fast. I didn't even get a turn!"

"Don't worry, there's more where that came from. Let's get dressed."

"Right behind you."

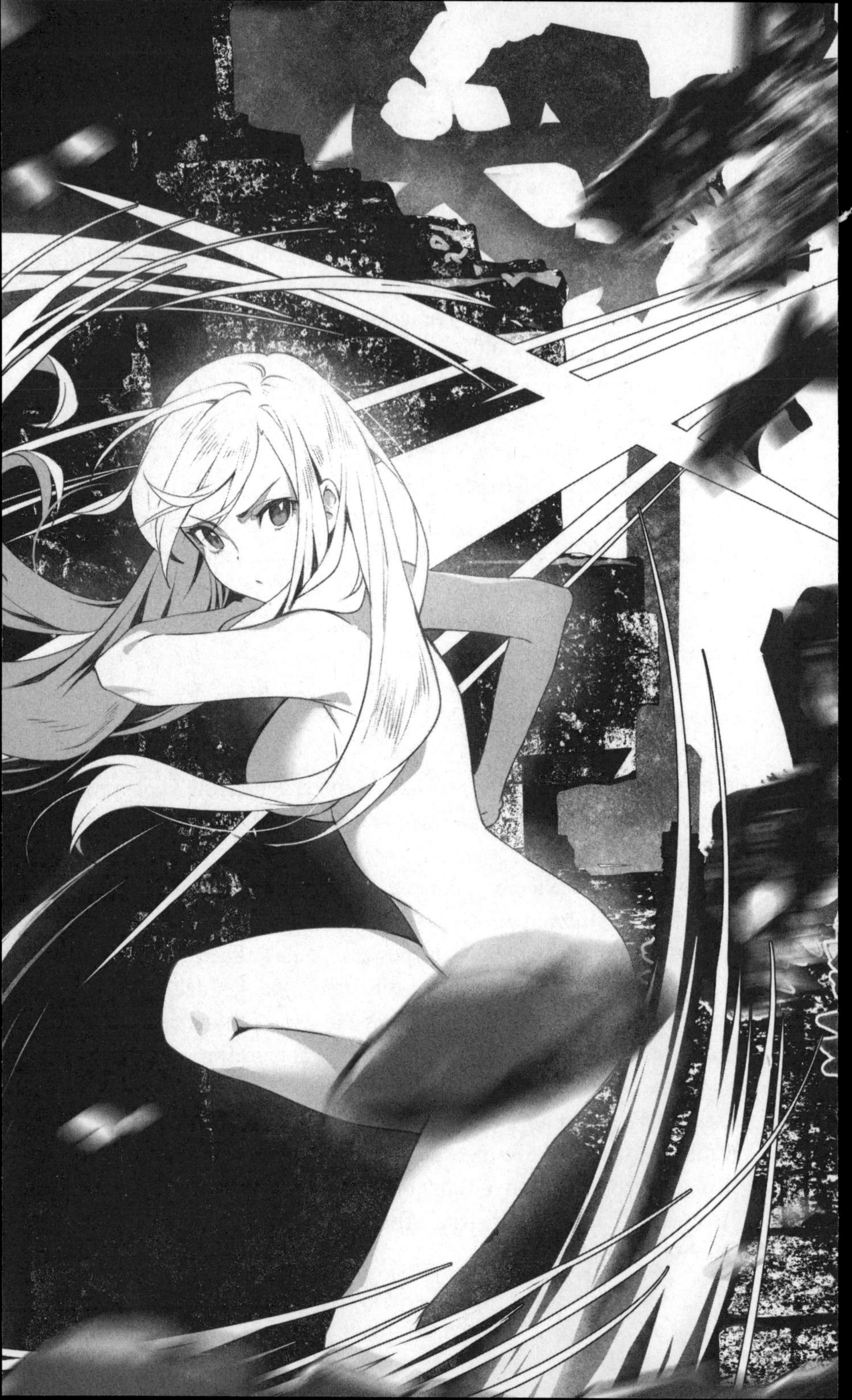

## Chapter VIII: Inglis, Age 15—The City Ruled by Highlanders (Part 2)

Once they were clothed, they jumped out from the hole in the ceiling. As they looked down at the manor, they saw a gigantic magicite beast resting on its haunches in the courtyard, surrounded by the bleeding forms of the knights it had taken down. It was humanoid, with wings on its back and a curve to its chest suggesting it had once been a woman. And from its forehead shone the stigmata of a Highlander.

"What?! There's no way!"

"No... That can't be Cyrene..." Rafinha's voice shook in horror.

◆◇◆

A flash of light flew from the extended palm of the beast, formerly Cyrene, turning to a blazing red as it burned through the manor's wall. Inglis recognized it as a beam of heat, and a powerful one at that. Flames sprung forth at its passage, and fire soon enveloped the manor as the beam carved through the knights trying to extinguish the inferno.

*At this rate...!*

"I can't believe Cyrene turned into a magicite beast..." Inglis whispered to herself.

As her mind raced, a memory drifted to the forefront of her thoughts: three years ago when the former holy knight Leon had turned Rahl into a magicite beast. She recalled the substance known as prism powder. That was what Leon had used to transform Rahl. Was this the same? Leon had said he'd received the powder from the Steelblood Front, anti-Highland guerillas.

"Is the Steelblood Front behind this?" she wondered aloud.

"You mean, like when Leon turned Rahl into a monster?" Rafinha asked.

"Yeah. I think that's what happened here." One thing still didn't make sense to Inglis, and she stood there, deep in thought. "But when could it have happened?"

The answer came as Inglis heard a woman's manic laugh from the courtyard below.

"Aha ha ha ha! Serves you right! We'll put an end to you Highlanders! My son was killed by one of you! I'll never, ever forgive you! Burn in hell!"

"Wait, is that Mimosa?!" Rafinha gasped.

"*She* did that to Cyrene?!" Could Mimosa be a Steelblood collaborator? Inglis wasn't sure, but something did come to mind. "That must be it! The herbal tea Mimosa served! It must have had prism powder in it!"

"Whaaat?!" Rafinha shouted in surprise.

Inglis thought back to what Leon had said. *Prism powder doesn't work on humans. That must be why it didn't affect me or Rafinha. Did Cyrene's innate trust in people let an enemy into her ranks?*

Inglis didn't think so. Cyrene was a perceptive woman. Even if it seemed like a dangerous plan, she may well have let her guard down around Mimosa precisely to unravel her hatred, hoping someday she'd understand. Inglis considered that too naive, though, if it had led to this.

"Aha ha ha ha ha!"

Cyrene fired a blast of heat at the laughing Mimosa, vaporizing her upper body as her legs fell to the ground. A swift, brutal end.

"Why? Why would she do all that, just to get herself killed?!" Rafinha shouted, tears in her eyes.

"Logic doesn't matter for grudges that deep."

"But Cyrene wasn't even the one who hurt her son!"

"Mimosa probably considered none of the Highlanders blameless."

"That's too tragic!"

"You may be right, but we can't focus on that right now. Let's stop Cyrene! I'll handle her. You go take on the other magicite beasts!"

"Okay," Rafinha said, trailing off before she asserted, "but please save her somehow. Please!"

"I'll try. Let's go."

Inglis and Rafinha leaped from the roof to the courtyard.

"Everyone, get out of here!" Inglis shouted, darting in front of Cyrene. "We'll deal with this!"

## Chapter VIII: Inglis, Age 15—The City Ruled by Highlanders (Part 2)

Rafinha loosed arrows of light at the magicite beasts as she called out. "Even if you're a knight, run away!"

Inglis was confident someone had fed the rats of the castle some prism powder as well. There weren't many left at this point; Rafinha could handle them on her own.

"Graaaaah!"

Cyrene let out a mournful cry as she turned her fist toward Inglis. Inglis stood still, awaiting the attack. *If I dodge, who knows where the beam will hit? Better to reduce the collateral damage by blocking it!*

"Haaaaaaaaah!" Inglis activated Aether Shell, and a cold light washed over her.

Cyrene retaliated with another beam of heat.

"Please, stop!" Inglis raised her hand to ward off the attack. As it met her hand, it twisted around and shot off into the sky. Without any special power, the pain would have been excruciating. Thankfully, she was able to wrap herself in aether and deflect the beams. Twice, then a third time, Cyrene fired at Inglis, but each beam twisted around the girl before disappearing into the starry yonder.

"Graaaaah!"

Next, Cyrene fired a fusillade aimed not at Inglis, but at the trees and buildings behind her, intending to bury her in rubble.

"Oh no you don't!" Before the beam could strike, Inglis threw herself in front of it. "Cyrene! If you can hear me, please stop!"

Cyrene replied with a broad spray of fire.

"Ngh! Haaaaaaaaah!" As an uncountable mass of beams sprayed forth, Inglis blocked each and every one in a display that looked less like combat and more like a beautiful but intense dance, like a goddess's reverie in the moonlight.

The knights were so entranced that, rather than fleeing, they stopped to stare.

"I-Incredible! She's amazing!"

"It's like there are dozens of her..."

"H-How beautiful. Am I dreaming?"

Inglis glanced over at the knights and shook her head. "Don't just stand around gawking! Get out of here!"

Inglis returned her focus to Cyrene as a golden spear pierced through the beast's shoulder. Rushing toward them was a beautiful, crimson-haired woman—the hieral menace Sistia.

Sistia sprung from the ground, striking again.

"Graaaaah!"

Cyrene roared in agony as the spear struck home. Purple blood erupted from the wound.

"Drop dead!" Sistia bellowed.

"Wait, stop!" Inglis dove, trying to stop the follow-up hail of thrusts from hitting Cyrene, and slammed Sistia into the wall.

"Ugh...?! What are you doing?! Stay out of my way! I didn't come here to fight you! Let me finish her off before this gets any worse!"

"You're with the Steelbloods, aren't you?"

"What's it matter to you?"

Inglis clenched her fist and grit her teeth. "If I had dealt with you then... Maybe I should now!" she growled.

A voice suddenly sounded from behind Inglis, and a black-gloved hand caught her wrist. "No, it wouldn't have changed anything. We always carry Prism Powder with us. Mimosa had it long before I arrived. This wasn't your fault."

Inglis whipped her head around to see a man.

"She moved on her own initiative after seeing the rebel knights fail," he continued, "no matter the cost to herself. I must admit—I admire her determination."

## Chapter VIII: Inglis, Age 15—The City Ruled by Highlanders (Part 2)

"Who the hell are you?!" Inglis shouted.

He was wearing a strange outfit: a black mask on his face and a black cloak on his body. Inglis only had his voice and build to go on, discerning he was a man from those alone. His voice, while muffled by the mask, sounded strangely familiar.

"I am the leader of the Steelblood Front," he announced. "I need no name. Call me what you will. I am here to protect this land." He had no need for further introduction.

"So you're protecting even the knights?" Inglis asked.

"Precisely. The...removal...of the Highlander was Mimosa's decision. No one else should suffer for it."

"And neither should Cyrene!"

"There is no way to return a magicite beast to what it once was. Or did you have some sort of plan?"

"I'm trying to figure that out now. So stay out of my way."

"I'm not here to play your game!" Sistia rushed at Cyrene again.

"Wait!" Inglis gave chase, only for the black-masked man to step between them. "Out of my way!"

Inglis wound up a strike, charged with her Aether Shell, to remove him from her path. It would be powerful enough to knock out even a hieral menace in one blow.

But he caught her fist.

The clang of hand on hand echoed all around them.

"Wh—?!"

"Ghhh—! Such a powerful blow!"

His hand bounced back, but that was all. Just a brush from his palm had absorbed all the energy Inglis put into her punch. This was the first time she had ever met someone who could take an Aether Shell-enhanced punch.

*There's still so much in this world I haven't seen. Even people like him!* It was a wonderful, fascinating realization. Every bit of her warrior's instinct was screaming out to her that this was her perfect opponent. Right now, though, she needed to stop Sistia! "Out of my way!"

"Sorry, but I can't let you do that!"

Inglis let loose a fierce flurry of blows, but the black-masked man was able to fend her off by focusing on his defense. Holding her at a standstill was enough to accomplish his goals.

Meanwhile, Sistia closed in on Cyrene. "Got you— Guh?!" Before she could land a blow, she was forced to evade a hail of arrows of light.

"I won't let you! Cyrene's my friend!" Rafinha had fired the volley which forced Sistia to hold back.

"Then I'll take you down first!" Sistia turned toward Rafinha.

Three new voices chimed in.

"Lady Cyrene!"

"Lady Cyrene, are you okay?!"

"What happened? Did you get hurt?"

Rino, Miyumi, and Chico—the adorable orphans Cyrene had taken in—were all crying out for her.

Inglis felt her heart race. *They still haven't evacuated?!*

The orphans recognized Cyrene even as a magicite beast and ran to her to see if she was okay. However, not even they were safe from the beast she had become.

"Rino! Miyumi! Chico! Run away!" Rafinha called out, her voice thick with worry.

"Curses! Sistia, save them!"

"Got it!" As fast as Sistia was, though, there was no way she could make it in time.

Cyrene's hand wavered, almost like she was trying to hold back, but that lasted only for a moment. She fired another beam—at herself.

"Ah—!" Inglis gasped.

That one motion told an entire story. Somewhere, deep inside, Cyrene was still Cyrene. Trying to protect the orphans, even if it meant taking her own life. She had said she wanted to protect the denizens of the surface. In the end, that was obviously true.

## Chapter VIII: Inglis, Age 15—The City Ruled by Highlanders (Part 2)

*The idea was so idealistic that I wasn't sure until now whether she meant it. But if she really is that kind of person, I can't let her die here!*

"Aether Pierce!" In no time at all, Inglis fired a concentrated shot of aether from her finger, striking Cyrene's palm and throwing off her aim. Cyrene's attack, the beam of heat, shot off into the sky.

"Hmm! Not bad!" the black-masked man said, impressed.

"Good job, Chris!" Rafinha cheered. She, no doubt, grasped onto this remaining chance for a happy enough ending.

"What are you doing?!" Sistia scowled at Inglis. "She was going to finish herself off! She knows what's best for her now. Just let her do it!"

Even ignoring Sistia, Inglis still didn't have a plan. However, she knew if she let Cyrene die, she'd regret it. Besides, she couldn't let that tragedy unfold in front of Rafinha. They had plans. They were going to have enough money to eat their way all the way to the capital! They were going to go see the frozen Prismer in Ahlemin! If Inglis didn't find a way to make this right, that happy future wouldn't be the same.

As Inglis thought, she had a flash of inspiration: *It may not solve everything, but it'll help!*

"I have an idea! Draw Cyrene's attention without hurting her! There's something I want to try! If it doesn't work, I won't stop you, okay?" Inglis called out to Sistia and the black-masked man.

"Who gave you the right to order me around?!" shot back Sistia.

"Wait, Sistia," he interrupted, extending an arm to hold her back. He turned to Inglis. "Hmmm… You may try it. But whether it works or not, you'll leave this town immediately. Do we have a deal? I don't want you interfering when we destroy the floating circle."

"Okay," Inglis said. "It's a pity we won't get to duel, though."

"A pity? I'd far rather fight side-by-side with you instead. Let's go, Sistia! Draw her attention without attacking for now!"

"Yes, sir!"

*It seems like Sistia's willing to trust his orders implicitly.* Inglis watched the hieral menace move without hesitation. *Cyrene should be safe while I try to make this work.*

"Chris! What are you doing? Can I help?"

"It's fine, Rafinha. You've already helped more than enough."

"What do you mean?"

"Watch, and you'll see. I'm going to stop Cyrene."

"Okay! Good luck, Chris!"

"Here I go!"

Inglis closed her eyes and focused. Just as she'd done before, she began to convert her aether into mana. Not just some of it, though—all of it. Every ounce of aether she could muster, transformed to mana!

"Haaaaaaaaah!" Streams of mana evaporated from her as she charged her power. It may have seemed like a waste, but she had more up her sleeve.

Ignoring her sudden exhaustion, Inglis moved on to the next step: controlling that mana. Runes were a way to control mana in a constant flow. Even modern humans, who couldn't sense or understand it, could harness that power so long as they had a Rune. Artifacts took that flow and let their wielders fight as if slinging magic—or at least that's what the ancients had called such a force. If Inglis could control the flow of her own mana, she could essentially do the same thing.

By twelve, Inglis had learned to convert her aether to mana. And these past few years, she'd been practicing using that mana. Aether was difficult to control, especially when balancing multiple manifestations. For example, she couldn't use Aether Strike while maintaining Aether Shell. But compared to aether, mana was weak and easy to control.

So maybe, just maybe, she could channel the mana she'd shed while maintaining the flow of aether. The thoughts of what momentary power she'd be able to bring to fruition had driven her earlier practice sessions. Watching Rafinha use her Artifact, she'd memorized carefully where the mana flowed and where it pooled. Then Inglis had tried over and over to replicate the process for herself.

It had taken nearly two years from her first attempt to her first success. The lowest-class Artifacts had the simplest flows, and that success had finally come with one. Now, she was approaching the abilities of a middle-class Artifact—not enough for a powerful effect like a Gift, but enough to manifest spurts of flame or shards of ice.

Inglis opened her eyes. Her mana-weaving was complete. Channeling the last of her aether into mana, she let loose!

"Freeze!"

*Crrrrrack!*

A cold wind swept through the courtyard as ice began to form around Cyrene's feet. In the blink of an eye, it washed over her now-gigantic body, freezing her completely in a block of ice.

"Phew, it worked." Inglis sighed in relief. Mana burned a lot more energy, for a lot smaller of an effect, than aether did. Creating that pillar of ice had taken nearly every bit of strength she could muster.

"A-Amazing! It's huge!" Rafinha exclaimed.

Sistia gasped. "That's tremendous..."

Even the black-masked man seemed impressed. "Remarkable, managing that with mana."

"Uh, Chris... I know that slowed her down, but will she be okay?"

"Magicite beasts are resilient. When the ice melts, she'll probably start moving again as if nothing happened. So let's move her somewhere far away. We can't let her stay here. Once we get her where she can't do any harm, we can—"

"I don't know if we *can* move something that big." Rafinha gaped at the huge block of ice. Doubt clouded her eyes.

Inglis sighed in exhaustion. "We don't exactly have a choice in the matter. Let me rest a little, and then I'll carry her."

"Are you sure you can manage it? We'd rather you were gone as soon as possible," the masked man interjected.

"You're just going to have to wait. Deal with it."

"How rude. I wasn't trying to needle you, I was going to make her more easy to carry."

"Hmm? How would you do that?"

"Just watch." The black-masked man approached the pillar of ice encasing Cyrene and brushed it with his hand.

Pale, bluish smoke began to rise from where his palm stroked the ice. As it faded into the night air, it began to glow...

Inglis's jaw gaped. "Aether?!" This was the first time she had encountered someone else who could manipulate aether. Was he a divine knight too? Even though becoming one required the patronage of a god?

So the gods still took mortal form and lived on this earth? She'd sensed their presence many times in her past life, but not once since being reborn. Apart from Alistia, who had made Inglis her divine knight and then granted her a second life, there were other gods as well. But a divine knight was half-human, half-god. Surely, if she focused, she could sense their presence watching over the world—yet not a whiff of it was to be found.

Had the world, and the people in it, been allowed to stand on their own two feet? Had they simply been abandoned? She didn't know, but the presence of another divine knight suggested that there was more to the story for her to learn.

What's more, the flows of aether around him were completely alien to Inglis—elaborate, even.

"If I sap the force of her aether without changing its composition, she'll keep her shape," he explained.

The rising columns of aether smoke exploded. Within the pillar of ice, Cyrene began to transform. Just as he'd said it would, the pillar began to shrink, without distorting.

"Ooh! Wow! She's tiny now!" It was hard to miss the relief in Rafinha's voice.

Inglis drew in her breath. "Amazing!" It was a level of control Inglis had no hope of replicating. Instead of controlling only his own aether, the black-masked man was able to reach out and weave that of the magicite beast and the ice block holding it in place. It was less an amputation and more like delicate cuts here and there, leaving their original forms intact. Something that would be impossible without seeing,

## Chapter VIII: Inglis, Age 15—The City Ruled by Highlanders (Part 2)

and comprehending, each of the complex flows of aether that made up a living thing.

In the end, a clump of ice containing the beast that was Cyrene, small enough to hold in the palm of one's hand, lay at the masked figure's feet. After he picked it up, he handed it to Inglis. "She should be easier to carry now. And with most of her aether scattered to the winds, it would be nearly impossible to restore her to her original form. This also means she won't be able to go on any more rampages."

"Don't take this as thanks, but I'm impressed. It's amazing that you were able to—"

"It would have been very difficult if her aether had not been held in place. I thank you for freezing her."

Inglis frowned. "Really, I wish I could do that."

"It's not a matter of power. The power advantage is all yours—my talent is more in technique. There's no way I could manage that sort of output."

"I want to have power *and* technique!"

"Ha ha. A bold ambition indeed! But off with you, before you decide that you don't negotiate with guerillas."

"But what of the people of the manor? What of the town?"

"Don't worry. We'll protect them. Our enemy is Highland and Highland alone."

"Understood."

"Then, until we meet again."

"As foes, hopefully." Inglis gave the black-masked man a challenging glare.

"The beauty of an angel, concealing something else indeed…" Even he seemed to be taken aback.

"Let's go, Rani." Inglis motioned. "We need to get Cyrene out of this ice."

"Yeah! Then…!" Rafinha curtsied slightly to the black-masked man, and hastily followed Inglis. She couldn't quite bring herself to thank the man who had supplied Mimosa the Prism Powder, but she was still relieved that, even after Cyrene's transformation, they'd been able to keep her alive.

◆◇◆

A short time later...
Departing Nova, Inglis and Rafinha made their way toward the capital. They had almost reached Ahlemin, where the frozen Prismer awaited them.

*Drip...drop...*

A drizzle of rain tickled Inglis's nose as she sat on the driver's bench. "Oh... It's raining."
Not the Prism Flow, just a normal rain. But it could change at any time. So it was best to stop and take shelter.
"It sure is! Let's wait it out, Chris!"
"Yeah. We can take shelter under that tree." Inglis turned their wagon toward a massive old tree. "Though it's no fun having to stop when we're so close to Ahlemin."
"Oh well. But we can afford to take it easy! There's still plenty of time until we have to be at the academy." Rafinha slouched onto the driver's bench. "Why don't we wrap ourselves in blankets and wait under the canopy? I don't want to catch a cold."
As Rafinha spoke, something began to squirm at the hemline of Inglis's top, and a face appeared from her cleavage—the tiny magicite beast Cyrene.
Shrunk by the black-masked man, she'd sprung back to life as soon as the ice melted. She was small, adorable—but still a magicite beast. She couldn't speak, and she was still aggressive. Nonetheless, she seemed to recognize Inglis and Rafinha and gradually grew accustomed to their presence. As they had continued their travels, this version of Cyrene had become something of a pet to them.

## Chapter VIII: Inglis, Age 15—The City Ruled by Highlanders (Part 2)

The two had taken to calling her Rin, a short version of Cyrene. And unfortunately for Inglis, she had decided on a favorite hiding place. Rafinha didn't provide quite enough reassuring shelter, but Inglis, on the other hand...

"Don't squirm like that, Rin. It tickles."

Rin tilted her head before burrowing again.

*Squirm, squirm, squirm!*

She burrowed even farther than before!

"Eek! Stop it, Rin! C'mon, Rani, make her stop!"

"Oh, I'd love to take over, but I can't disturb her when she's so comfy. Keep up the good work, Chris!"

"C'mon, have a little sympathy!"

As Rin gradually calmed down, Rafinha's impish grin faded, and she sighed.

"What's wrong, Rani?"

"Hey, Chris. Rin was a really good person when she was Cyrene, right?"

"Yes, she was."

"But her superiors in Highland wanted to take the whole town for themselves?"

"Precisely. She wanted to stop them."

"Didn't the Steelbloods say they were going to protect Nova?"

"Well, they said they were going to destroy the floating circle."

"I can't even tell what's right or wrong anymore. It's all so confusing."

"Sounds like this is a part of growing up."

"Is this really what it's like? Don't you... Aren't you worried about it?"

"Not really. I'm not going to think about it too hard. If I focus on getting stronger, what is there to worry about? How about you, Rani?"

"Aha ha ha. That's exactly the kind of thing I expected you to say. That's not really like me, though."

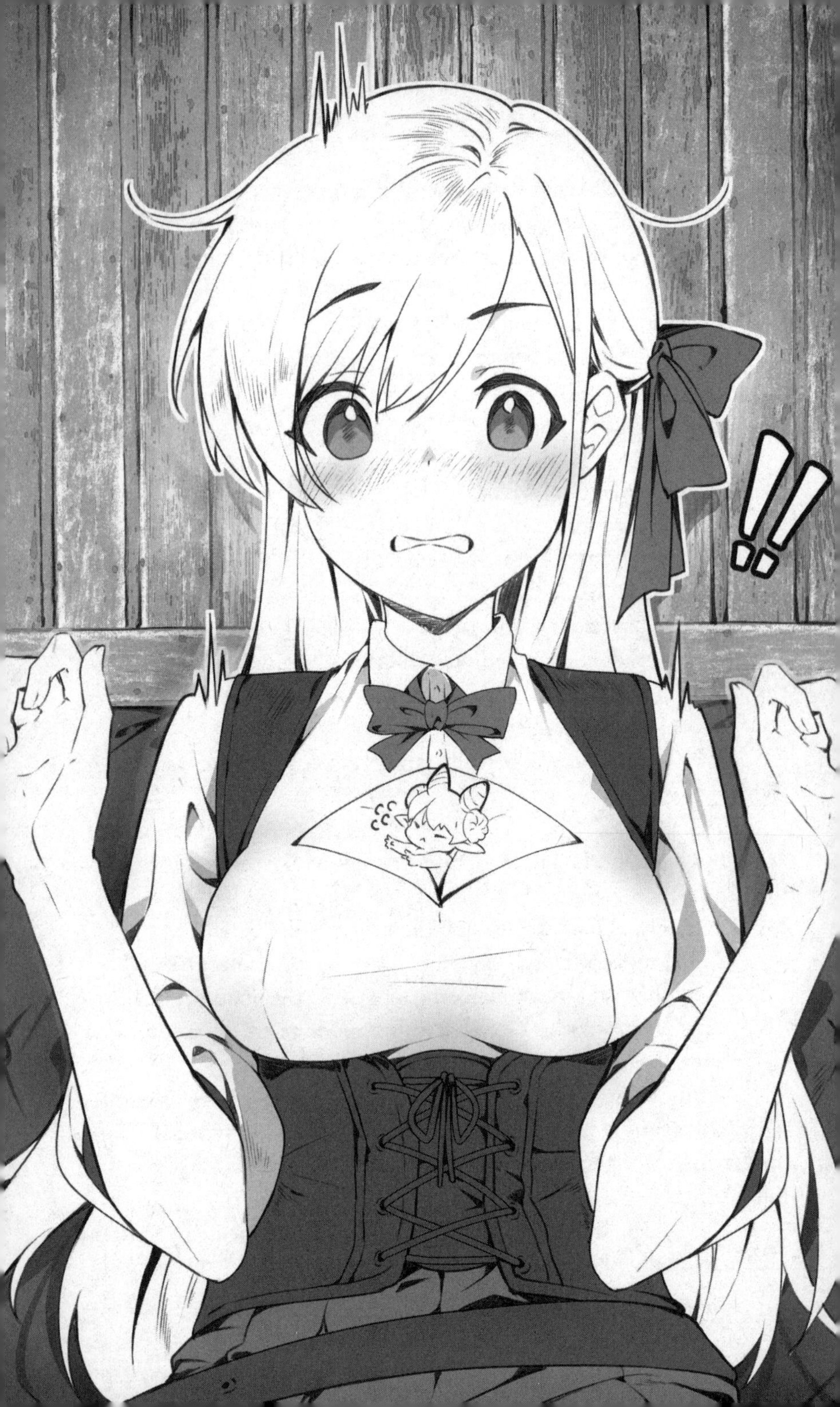

"Then worry all you want. I'll always be there for you." Inglis reached over and stroked Rafinha's hair.

"Mm... Thanks."

Eventually, the rain passed, and Inglis and Rafinha arrived at Ahlemin.

# Chapter IX: Inglis, Age 15— The Rimebound Prismer

In the center of Ahlemin stood a cathedral as large as any castle, inside of which was the frozen corpse of a Prismer. When one of these ultimate magicite beasts had been slain, its carcass remained where it had fallen, with none able to move it. At first, Ahlemin was nothing more than the barricades around the Prismer, then it housed a force to keep careful watch, and finally it became a city to support the people keeping watch.

Intense as the guard was, though, visitors could still obtain permission to enter. Because Rafinha was not only the daughter of Duke Bilford but also the sister of the holy knight Rafael, that permission was forthcoming—for herself and for her loyal squire, Inglis.

Rafinha stared at the wings of the birdlike beast glimmering above. "Wow! So that's a Prismer. It looks so tough!"

As gigantic as Rahl or Cyrene had become, this was nearly ten times larger. The scale of the cathedral, already an imposing building from outside, was truly revealed only when seeing the massive pit within built to encircle the Prismer. The exterior construction was a small portion of the building as a whole.

As for the Prismer, the scars of its last battle dotted its wings, its legs, and its body.

Even still, within the ice, Inglis could sense a strange power pulsating. *Maybe it's not quite dead. I can't say for sure, not having seen it alive, but...*

Rafinha pouted. "C'mon, Chris. Could you stand to look a little less excited? People are gonna think you're weird."

Access to the cathedral was restricted to high-ranking knights, highborn nobility, and kingdom officials—in other words, the ruling class—solely for them to take in the full menace of a Prismer. They would feel their hair stand on end but turn their horror into determination in the end. The visit was supposed to bestow a somber awe of the foe they might face one day.

*Somber* being the intention.

Yet here was Inglis, decked out in her formal best, staring up at the Prismer, her eyes sparkling with admiration and anticipation. A reaction like that was sure to draw the attention of the knights on duty.

"It's incredible!" Inglis exclaimed in wonder. "I'd love the chance to fight it. I wonder if it'll ever thaw out like Rin did."

That very same Rin nervously peeked out from the neckline of Inglis's shirt, instinctively terrified of the Prismer.

"Really, Chris. This place is under a super-tight watch. If you keep being weird, they're gonna haul you off."

"But, but—! Frozen or no, can't you feel the power it emanates? It might still be alive. Someone should crack it out of there and finish it off. And ideally, that someone should be me."

"Seriously, Chris—"

"You there!" One of the knights guarding the cathedral suddenly called out.

"Eeek?! Oh, aha ha ha, just ignore her," Rafinha said with her cutest smile. "She's an oddball. I mean, you see how cute she is, right? You know how the good-looking ones get sometimes. But don't worry! I'll keep an eye on her!"

The knight shook his head. "Uh, I don't quite follow, but there are magicite beasts loose in the town! It's dangerous. You need to stay in the cathedral until things calm down. This is the safest place to be."

## Chapter IX: Inglis, Age 15—The Rimebound Prismer

Inglis grinned. "Magicite beasts? I can hear my fists calling out to me!"

She rushed off toward the cathedral's entrance. Seeing the Prismer had worked up her fighting spirit. Magicite beasts were not as fun to clash with, but they were better than nothing.

"Hey, wait!" the knight yelled at Inglis, who ignored him without a second thought.

"Sheesh! Chris! This really doesn't seem like a good idea." Rafinha paused. "But what the heck—I'm in!"

More hands in a fight wouldn't hurt. Besides, hiding inside when people were in danger wasn't something Rafinha's morals could allow.

She turned to the knight with a nod as she followed Inglis. "Sorry, but we're gonna go help! Thanks for telling us about it, though!"

As Inglis left the cathedral, she saw the horde of magicite beasts descending upon the city. Most were soaring through the air above like birds or perched on rooftops. However, as numerous as they were, so were the knights who battled against them. It was, after all, a city founded to keep watch over the dead Prismer. It would naturally be well-defended.

As she ran out through the streets, Inglis hunted for a target.

*Take a right, and through to that plaza!* she thought as she sprinted ahead. She came out to an open space and saw about ten magicite beasts in the form of flightless birds milling about. It was the closest place with a good selection of foes, and a squad of knights had already formed a battle line and were closing in slowly.

"Not if I beat you to the punch!" Inglis broke into a sprint and leaped over them in a flash, eager to take on the magicite beasts alone.

The knights screamed at her in panic. To them, all they saw was a kid rushing headfirst into certain death.

"Whoa! Wha—?! No!"

"What are you doing?! It's dangerous!"

"Wait, there's too many! Stop! Get back here!"

"Thanks, but I'll be fine." Inglis flashed a grin. If nothing else, she appreciated their concern.

A shadow darted out from the sidewalk, grabbing Inglis and pulling her to the ground. "You fool! What are you doing?!"

"Aaah?!"

Inglis was shocked; she hadn't expected anyone to take her unawares, whether or not she was using aether.

*Who is this? They're not half bad.*

Inglis took a good look at the new threat, a girl of around her own age with deep indigo hair.

"You don't have a Rune or an Artifact, and you're taking on a pack of magicite beasts? Are you trying to get yourself killed?!" the girl yelled. "You're beautiful! Don't throw your life away!"

The girl lecturing Inglis was beautiful in her own right. Her stern face was offset by fashionable ribbons on either side, and she was voluptuous, with a chest comparable to Inglis's, maybe even larger—the kind Rin would probably love to nest in. And as could be expected of someone willing and capable of stopping Inglis, her hand bore a black Rune in the shape of a greatsword, matching the slab of metal strapped to her back. It was an upper-class one, theoretically on par with Rafinha's. She must have been an upper-class *knight*. It was a rare sight, even for Inglis.

"Thanks again, but really, I'll be fine," Inglis insisted.

"Here they come! Get back!" The girl stepped forward, shielding Inglis from the beasts.

Their attention well and truly drawn, the magicite beasts began to swarm the two in leaps and bounds, ready to use their speed and weight to crush their foes. Yet the girl with the Rune held firm, as if the odds only steeled her resolve.

"I can take them out just fine myself!" In a fluid motion, she unslung her greatsword and leveled it at the beasts. She swept the blade sideways before they had a chance to draw close.

Curious, Inglis watched quietly rather than competing for prey.

"Line 'em up—" The girl's sword glowed and then extended, quickly becoming long enough to connect with its intended targets. "—and cut

## Chapter IX: Inglis, Age 15—The Rimebound Prismer

'em down!" The extended blade continued through its arc, slashing cleanly through the beasts' necks.

"Huh, I've never seen that before," Inglis said, impressed.

*Transforming like that must be that Artifact's gift*, she thought. *There's probably a lot of ways you could take advantage of that. I've been wanting a weapon of my own lately, so honestly, I'm kind of jealous.*

As Inglis reflected, the girl turned back to her. "Are you okay? You need to get out of—"

From over the girl's shoulder, Inglis saw a flock of birdlike magical beasts swoop down from the rooftops. The creatures craned their necks to inhale deeply before blasting forth a storm of bladelike hail. Inglis didn't find that surprising for a magicite beast. Rin was able to shoot white-hot beams from her hands too.

"Behind you! A blizzard!" Inglis yelled.

At Inglis's warning, the girl spun around on a heel and planted her greatsword in the ground. "As if!"

The sword didn't just lengthen, but it also expanded several times, enough for her and Inglis to take cover behind.

The hail pelted off the blade of the greatsword, leaving the pair behind it completely unharmed.

That the technique could be used both offensively and defensively did not escape Inglis's notice.

"My turn now!" the mysterious girl declared.

The storm passed, and she went on the counterattack. Facing a beast on a nearby roof, she sent the tip of her sword plunging forward toward the beast. Inglis didn't know if the girl didn't quite have the reach or if the beast was exceptionally nimble. It flitted out of the way.

"Hmph. Cheeky one, aren't you!"

"I'll help out. Sit still for a second," Inglis whispered to the girl before jumping onto the blade of the sword and sprinting to the roof.

"Whaaa—?! What the heck?! You're fast!" she gasped in shock.

Inglis, closing in on the beast, took a running leap from the roof. She tumbled forward, slamming her heel into its head.

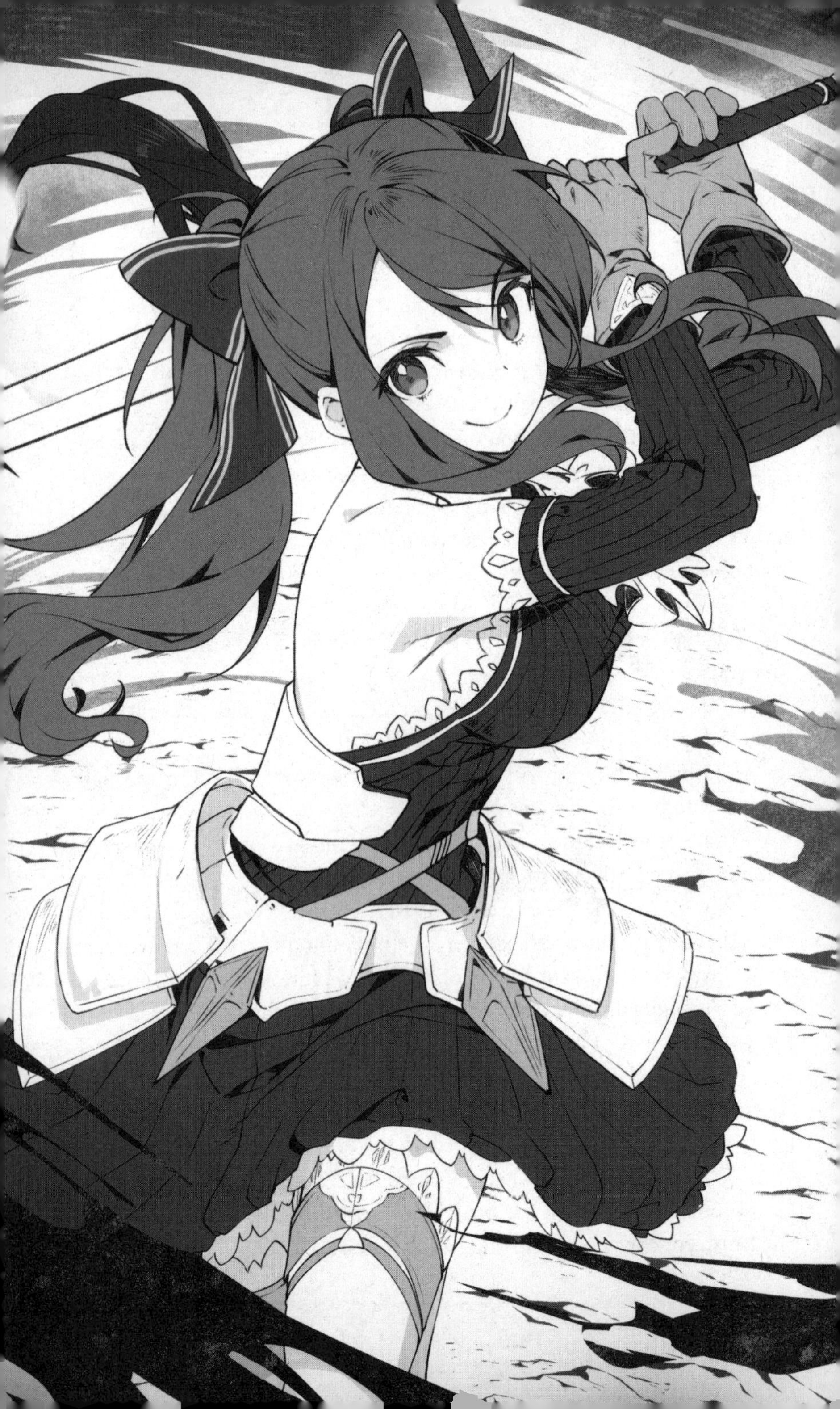

## Chapter IX: Inglis, Age 15—The Rimebound Prismer

\* \* \*

"Cawwwwwwww?!"

As the beast plummeted toward the square, Inglis called out to the girl below. "Now! Slice it!"

"Got it!" The girl's swing was well-placed; it cleaved the beast in half.

"More are coming!" Inglis smashed a second, then a third, beast down toward the girl, who carved through them as they fell. "Not bad!" Inglis called over.

The girl beamed in return. "Same goes for you! I was worried about you when I didn't see a Rune or Artifact, but I guess I didn't need to get in your way. Sorry."

"No, I appreciate it."

"What's your name?"

"Inglis Eucus."

"I'm Leone. Leone Olfa. Let's team up for now."

*Olfa... That name sounds familiar.* Inglis shook her head. *I can worry about that after we take down the magicite beasts.* "Anyway, that sounds great, Lady Olfa."

"Call me Leone. We're around the same age, right?"

"Sure, Leone. Let's do this!"

"Yeah!"

The two exchanged smiles and set to driving the magicite beasts out of the city. Leone focused on ground combat, scything through the ostrich-like beasts. Meanwhile, Inglis took to the rooftops, smashing the flying beasts down for Leone to finish off.

The arrows of light shot by Rafinha's Artifact could easily take out slow-footed allies or the surrounding buildings, so Inglis thought the more precise control of Leone's Artifact seemed more suited to close fighting.

Cutting through Inglis's contemplation was a trio of flying beasts crowded on the roof of a nearby shop. She launched herself toward them.

"One!"

After making landfall on the roof, Inglis sprung up again, slamming her foot through a roundhouse kick into the neck of a beast.

As another pecked toward her back, she let her momentum carry her around fully, slipping past its attack before she grabbed it by the neck and swung it into the third.

"Two!"

The beast, caught by the full weight of Inglis's second foe, fell like a rock toward Leone.

"Three!"

Inglis immediately slung along the beast in her grasp behind it—a little too early. Leone had cut two of the beasts down, but she was still in the process of winding up again for the last one.

"Oh! Sorry!"

"Aaaaaah! Too fast, Inglis!"

As Leone flailed her sword around in a fluster, an arrow of light flew past her, twisting around her to strike the beast down as it fell.

"Yay! A direct hit!" a familiar voice cheered. "Ugh, *really*, Chris! You can't run off like that. You left me behind."

"Rani! Good job catching up with us despite everything."

"It's not like you two were being all that stealthy." Rafinha looked over at Leone.

"She's Leone," Inglis said. "We happened to run into each other, and now we're fighting together."

"Nice to meet you. Thanks for covering me." Leone nodded to Rafinha.

"Pleased to meet you too! I'm Rafinha Bilford."

As Rafinha shot her a friendly smile, Leone gasped. "Bilford...? Rafinha? You're Rafael's sister?!"

"Oh! You know Rafael?"

"Yes. I owe him a lot."

"Let's talk about that later!" Inglis interrupted. "We've got magicite beasts to fight!"

With Rafinha there, Inglis's party blew through the magicite beasts.

## Chapter IX: Inglis, Age 15—The Rimebound Prismer

Barely an hour later, they had repelled every single beast there and returned peace to the city.

Rafinha ran the back of her hand over her brow. "Phew. That seems like about enough. Inglis, Leone, you must both be pretty tired out."

"Yeah." Leone nodded. "We were able to take a lot of them down because of you two, though. Thanks."

"Hmm." Rafinha paused to think. "But it's strange how they appeared here, like, out of nowhere. This town is heavily guarded. I guess it would make sense if the Prism Flow suddenly fell here, but…"

"You're right. Hmm, I wonder what happened."

"It's been happening a lot lately," Leone said. "Beasts suddenly show up in Ahlemin, even without the Prism Flow."

Inglis cut in enthusiastically. "At least there's never a dull moment."

"Huh? Um…" Leone was a bit taken aback.

"Oh, don't worry about her," Rafinha said. "She's got the body of an angel, but the soul of a warlord."

"Aha ha ha. But she calms right down as soon as the battle's over."

"Oh, do I, now." Inglis stared at Rafinha in response.

"Yeah! You only get worked up like that in a fight, Chris."

Leone nodded. "Now that I think of it, the first time I saw her, she *was* charging straight at a pack of magicite beasts. I was shocked."

"Yep, that's Chris for you. She really has a flair for making a first impression. I mean, a girl with no Rune running headfirst into battle? You'd think she'd get herself killed, right?"

"I tackled her to try to stop her before I even realized what I was doing! Turns out I didn't need to, though."

Inglis smiled as she listened to Rafinha and Leone. *If they get along this well, I'm not unhappy that we met.*

"You there! The dark-haired girl and the platinum blonde!" a middle-aged knight called out. "Thank you for helping defend the town! We'd like to reward you. Come with me."

Rafinha frowned. "Huh? But what about Leone? We weren't the ones who did most of the work—it was her."

Inglis, too, cocked an eyebrow at the knight.

"What? No, of course not! We have not a crumb for that traitor's blood!" The knight spoke as if surprised, and not a little offended, at the idea.

"Now hold on just a minute! You saw how hard she was fighting!" Rafinha refuted.

Leone spoke quietly. "Don't worry about me, Rafinha. You two go along with him."

"No! That's not right!"

The knight sounded indignant. "How could we trust someone like her? You two must not know who she is. She's Leone Olfa, sister of the traitor holy knight Leon Olfa! There can be no honor for one whose family scorns everything we hold dear!"

Rafinha's jaw dropped. "Whaaaat?!"

"I see." Inglis paused. She suddenly remembered something. "Leon was an Olfa..."

She had heard the name Olfa before in regard to Leon, the holy knight who turned to the Steelbloods.

"Now that you know, you'd best keep your distance. If you keep company like that, people will start to wonder why." The knight turned forward. "Let's go."

"Who cares about your reward, then! We don't need it!" Rafinha stuck out her tongue at the knight in a rather unladylike display.

"Let's get out of here." Inglis took Leone's hand and led her along the road.

"That's right!" Rafinha took her other hand.

A tear began to well up in the corner of Leone's eye as the two led her along. "Thank you."

Rafinha was still outraged. "What's wrong with them?! That's a terrible way to treat someone!"

Inglis agreed. "Yeah. Anyway, let's find somewhere calmer to talk."

Leone, gazing at the pavement, mumbled, "How about my house? It's not very fancy, but if we're outside like this..."

## Chapter IX: Inglis, Age 15—The Rimebound Prismer

"In that case, thank you for the invitation." Rafinha smiled.

"Yeah. Let's go get the wagon," Inglis suggested.

Once the trio returned to the wagon, Leone climbed in for the ride to her house.

Inglis called back to her from the driver's bench. "Are the people here always like that?"

"Yeah. Ever since Leon turned to the Steelbloods three years ago…"

"But you still fight for them?" Rafinha asked out of curiosity.

"Whatever differences we have, a magicite beast's a magicite beast."

"Wow, you're so mature! I'm impressed!" Rafinha's eyes gleamed as she grasped Leone's hand.

"Ha ha ha. I don't think I'm anything special. If nothing else, maybe someday they'll forgive me a little this way."

"They still shouldn't talk about you like that. You're fighting hard to protect them. They're so petty."

"Try not to blame them, though," Leone said. "They had a lot of hope riding on Leon—and a lot of respect for him. This town exists to watch over the dead Prismer, so there are many knights and a firm loyalty to the crown. Leon was the first holy knight we've ever had. So when he killed the inspector and the Highland ambassador and fled, his betrayal hurt all the more. They say the greatest hate springs from the greatest love."

"Huh? Wait, Lord Shiony was—" Rafinha said, but Inglis cut her off and leaned into her ear.

"The official story ended up being that it was all Leon's fault," Inglis whispered. "If people heard that it had been Rahl who killed Shiony, it would just drum up more support for anti-Highland movements, and opposition to the royals that yield to their demands. It was a more convenient explanation."

"But isn't it unfair to blame Leon for everything? Especially when all he did was not put up with Rahl's arrogance any longer."

"Wait, you two met Leon?"

"Yeah. He was friendly," Rafinha answered. "I don't think he was a bad person."

"I agree with Rani," Inglis added.

"I see." Leone took a moment to let their comments sink in. "Thanks. But don't worry about it. Even Prince Wayne and Rafael came to explain and apologize."

Inglis went over her picture of national politics. *Wayne... Right, that's the prince. He must be Rafael's commander.*

"I knew at least Rafael would be better," Rafinha said. "Really, though. This isn't right. Everyone else needs to at least apologize too."

"They checked in on me from time to time afterward, so I don't hold a grudge or anything. And plus...I mean, no matter what happened, Leon did abandon his rank and his country. The people have plenty of reasons to resent him. So it's up to me to restore honor to the Olfa name. Becoming a knight in my own right and capturing my brother should do it." Leone's eyes shone with determination.

"You're strong, Leone. There's a lot I could learn from you." Rafinha made no effort to hide her admiration.

Inglis, meanwhile, latched onto something else. "So you're not a knight yet, Leone?"

"That's right. Soon I'll be heading off to the academy. With my father gone now, there's nothing keeping me here."

"Wow, really?! Us too! We're on our way to the knights' academy ourselves!" Rafinha cheered.

"You are? Great! It'll be so nice to have classmates that—"

"This is a heck of a coincidence, but yeah! I can't wait!"

"Me too!" Inglis chimed in happily.

"Me three, then!"

The trio held hands, excitedly looking forward to their future together.

"Ah, Rin!" Rin stuck her face out from Rafinha's shadow, then ran to Leone as fast as her tiny legs could carry her.

"Oh, my. Isn't she cute? I've never seen anything like her, though."

"She's Rin. She's our pet."

## Chapter IX: Inglis, Age 15—The Rimebound Prismer

Rin spun around in a circle in front of Leone, obviously also happy to meet her—just before diving down her shirt headfirst.

"Eeek! Where's she trying to— Ahh, stop it! What are you doing?!"

"Ah, Rin! Sorry, she loves to hide in places like that."

Inglis sighed in relief. "Phew. At least it's not just me anymore." Another reason for Inglis to be happy that Leone was there.

As Rin calmed down, Rafinha shined a smile at them. "Anyway, it sounds like we'll have a lot of fun at the academy."

"I'm still worried about how magicite beasts are appearing in town, though. I wish I could find out why before leaving," Leone remarked pensively.

"Do you have any leads to work with?" Inglis asked.

"Some rumors say it's because of the dead Prismer; others think it's something the Steelbloods are up to. There are a lot of explanations. I kind of lean toward the Steelbloods. If it was the Prismer, you'd think this sort of thing would have happened earlier."

Rafinha cupped her chin. "Hmmm. What do you think, Chris?"

"I don't think it's the Steelbloods. They didn't seem to care about anything but taking down the Highlanders, and there's not a consul here for them to go after. So what would be in it for them?"

Leone nodded. "I guess that's true. So then it probably is the Prismer."

"But it wasn't happening before?" Rafinha asked.

"I know we only recently arrived," Inglis said, "but I don't think that Prismer's dead. And if it isn't, I wouldn't be surprised if it could summon lesser magicite beasts."

"What?! You can tell it's alive, Inglis?!"

"I think it's alive, at least."

"Hmm." Leone paused in thought. "What could we even do about that, then?"

"Thaw it out and kill it for real. I wish they'd let me give it a try." Inglis sighed like a young maiden in love.

Leone and Rafinha turned to each other in quiet conversation. "Uh, Rafinha, she's kind of creeping me out."

"I know, right? But it's nothing new. She's always like this."

◆ ◇ ◆

Following Leone's directions, they arrived at a mansion with intricate outer walls. Its courtyard, however, was a blighted, bare space, stripped of the verdant landscaping one would expect of such a residence.

"I know it's a bit rude to point this out, but it seems kind of…desolate here."

"Yeah. You're right, Rani."

"A little while ago, a mob stormed up here from town to punish our family," Leone said. "The building was fine, but the garden burned away. We didn't bother replanting. If we fixed things up, it'd only make them want to tear things down again. I'm sorry it looks so uninviting from the outside, but indoors, the hearth's still burning. Not that anyone is here to tend it but myself."

"It's fine," Inglis said. "That means you don't have to worry about anyone else, right?"

"Thanks for your understanding," Leone said after a pause.

She pulled the gates to the courtyard open.

*Whoosh!*

A loud noise passed over their heads. Inglis looked up to see a small, winged ship made of iron. Its complicated mechanisms made it obvious that it was not built on the surface, but rather a gift from Highland.

*This must be a Flygear,* Inglis thought.

This particular example was a standing type, with birdlike wings on either side of a metal hull that held a control stick and bars for the riders to grip. The hull was small, affording room for perhaps one or two

## Chapter IX: Inglis, Age 15—The Rimebound Prismer

passengers alongside its pilot. The Flygear was a new type of aircraft that Highland only recently sent down; it was still rare on the surface. Inglis could count the number of times she'd seen one out as far as Ymir on her fingers.

Uniquely, though, a Flygear required the involvement of a knight and their Rune to charge. Once powered, though, the Rune was no longer necessary to control its flight. Meaning a certain Runeless squire was still fully qualified to pilot one.

The term *knight* may have sprung into existence referring to heavy cavalry, but a squire on a Flygear was surely the equal of a knight on horseback. That'd make magicite beasts easier to deal with and allow for rapid tactical changes in redeploying forces. With dispersed forces that could concentrate quickly at a focal point, knights and their squires could more effectively fulfill their mission of protecting humans from magicite beasts. That was definitely a development Inglis was pleased with.

The knights' academy, which was at the forefront of developing the doctrine for that mission, had recently instituted a course for squires for the development of a corps of trained Flygear pilots. It was the academy's decision that a knight should focus on the training and use of their Artifact for battle, while Runeless squires would pilot the Flygears. That would make forces the most efficient.

Inglis herself, of course, was destined for that squires' course and expected to become quite familiar with a Flygear's handling. And if the current strategic thinking held, she'd be paired up with an Artifact-wielding knight, almost certainly Rafinha.

"A Flygear's landing!" she announced.

The ornithopter slowly descended into the courtyard of Leone's mansion. As it came level with the ground, its two passengers popped into view. The first was a short-statured yet curvy girl with auburn hair. Her eyes gleamed with a curiosity almost as intense as Rafinha's, and her doglike animal ears and tail marked her as a demihuman. The second was a tall young man in his early twenties with black hair. His face was handsome, gentle but with a sharp focus.

*Ah! He's grown up so well!* Inglis thought as she stared at her cousin, Rafinha's brother, Rafael.

"Oh, isn't that—Rafael! Rafaeeel!" As soon as Rafinha recognized her brother, she ran up to the Flygear and dove to embrace him as it landed.

"Wha—?! Rani?! It's really you, Rani! What on earth are you doing here? How have you been?"

"Just fine! We came to see the dead Prismer here on our way to the capital! Chris just couldn't miss the chance!"

"I see. So Chris is with you?"

"Yes. It's a pleasure to see you again." Inglis had followed hot on Rafinha's heels, and gave a quick curtsy as Rafael's focus swung to her.

Rafael was stunned into silence for a moment. "Wow. Y-You're beautiful! I didn't realize—"

Inglis was fifteen years old, but she'd been an early bloomer and looked seventeen or eighteen—enough to stand out as a woman, at least. Rafael seemed a little bit nervous as he looked at her.

*He's grown up in a lot of ways, but definitely not all of them.*

The girl who'd accompanied him on the Flygear teased the young holy knight. "Why, I thought I'd never see the day! Rafael blushing at a girl? Is the legendary wallflower finally blossoming?!"

"S-Stop it, Ripple!"

"Thank you, Rafael." Inglis knew she looked good and wasn't particularly averse to having it recognized, but she really would have preferred if he had immediately unsheathed his sword with a *It's been so long since we've had a chance to spar!* instead. As a smile spread across her face at the thought, Rafael smiled in return.

"Yeah. I'm glad to see you again too, Chris."

Inglis turned to the other person from the Flygear. "And she's Ripple... The hieral menace Ripple?"

"Yeppers, that's me! Nice to meet ya!" Ripple beamed at Inglis.

"Did you come here to see Leone, Rafael?" Rafinha asked.

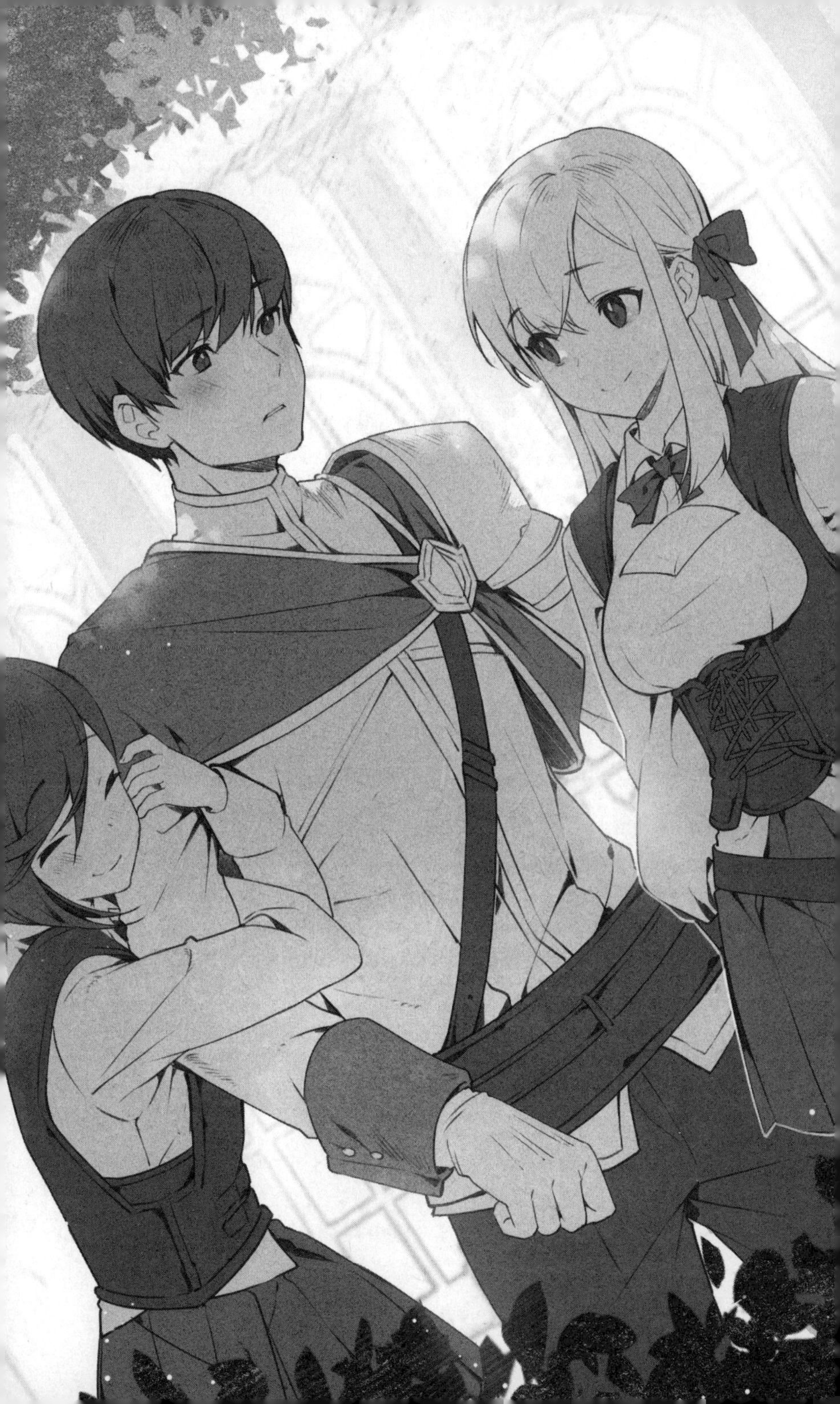

"Yeah. I was already in the area for a mission, so I thought I'd drop in."

"Oh? What mission are you on?"

"Well..." he said before trailing off. "Actually, I bet we're all pretty hungry. Why don't we talk over a meal?"

Rafinha definitely was. "I'm famished! How about you, Chris?"

"Sure am."

"Why don't we head inside, then? I'll whip something up—" Leone began to offer, only for Rafael to shake his head.

"That won't—"

Rafinha cut in. "It probably—no, it definitely won't—"

"It won't be enough." Inglis finished for the three of them.

"Why don't you come along with us, Leone? I'll rent a space, so you don't have to worry about standing out," Rafael offered.

Under his command now, Inglis and the others moved out to dinner.

◆◇◆

After Rafinha gave a brief narrative of the events at Nova, Rafael was relieved that she and Inglis had made it out unharmed.

"So that's what happened in Nova, then. I'd heard rumors that the consul had gone missing, but that really must have been tough for the two of you. I'm glad you came back safe from meeting the leader of the Steelbloods."

Inglis was curious if he knew more about what had happened there. "What I'm really worried about is the floating circle. Did the king know about that when he handed over the town to Highland?" *If he did, that means he really did abandon his people.*

"Well, it's the first I've heard of it. I can't speak for his close advisers, though."

Rafinha pouted. "If he did, I'm gonna be so angry."

Chapter IX: Inglis, Age 15—The Rimebound Prismer

"Me too, Rani," Rafael said. "Thanks, Rani. Thanks, Chris. That's really important information. Thank you for telling me."

That was enough to ease Rafinha's worry for now. "Mm. I hope it comes in handy."

"You're welcome." Inglis agreed.

Rafael had his own questions. "What really surprises me is that, even after the consul became a magicite beast, you were able to tame her."

"Well, she was a Highlander rather than an animal or insect beforehand, and an exceptionally thoughtful one on top of that," Inglis explained. "I wonder if there's still some bit of that left, struggling against a magicite beast's instincts."

"Maybe it has something to do with her being so tiny."

"Hmmm."

Leone's and Ripple's eyes were gradually widening as the conversation went on. They hadn't said a word.

The cousins had, between them, already polished off enough food to sustain a grown man for two or three days, and the empty plates were beginning to stack high on the table. They were nowhere near done yet either—even the conversation about Rin was taking place around half-chewed mouthfuls.

Ripple watched in incredulity. "Wow, I had no idea your sister and cousin were just as hungry as you."

"You all weren't kidding," Leone said. "There really wasn't enough food at my place to feed you."

As Rafinha marched her way through a third helping of steamed chicken, she asked her brother, "So, what are you doing here?"

"We were sent to help clear out the magicite beasts that suddenly appeared."

"That's been on my mind, too. I was thinking I should do something about it before leaving for the academy," Leone said, her voice growing quieter by the end.

"It'll be fine, Leone. A few more days, and it'll stop."

Inglis's brow furrowed. "Do you have something planned, Rafael?"

"I do. I believe their appearance is tied to the influence of the frozen Prismer. So..." Rafael's face was stone-serious as he explained, even with a piece of chicken tucked in his cheek.

Several days later...

Inglis, Rafinha, and Leone, along with Rafael and Ripple, soared through the sky aboard a Flygear Port, a sort of mothership for Flygears. It was a winged, barrel-like flying hull peppered with holes in which Flygears could land.

It was more than a storage hangar, though. Each of the docked Flygears also was a part of the Flygear Port's motive force. The common strategy for operations established a squadron of Flygears around a Flygear Port.

"If the frozen Prismer is creating magicite beasts, then moving it away from the town should prevent them from appearing there," Rafael had said to them during dinner a few nights ago.

That very plan was taking place before Inglis's eyes. The roof of Ahlemin's cathedral had been removed, and countless wires hung down and wrapped around the Prismer, allowing the Flygear Port and a large force of Flygears to begin lifting it away.

In other words, it was an airlift on a massive scale. The incredible sight of hundreds of Flygears spreading their wings was commanded by none other than the young holy knight Rafael, with the hieral menace Ripple there for backup.

Rafinha gasped. "This is amazing! I had no idea you could do even this with Flygears."

Rafael nodded. "Yeah. Flygears are so useful. Highland uses them too. Having some of our own gives us more options."

"Even if the Steelbloods were behind the beasts, the Prismer is probably still involved, so I guess if it's gone..." Leone continued to be the most suspicious of the Steelbloods, but that was enough of an explanation for her.

One problem remained: if they were moving the Prismer, where were they moving it to? Dropping it in another town would just recreate the same problem there. Fortunately, there were other options.

"Moving it to an isolated area on a hostile border will let any magicite beasts it produces be our first line of defense," Inglis said. "Fighting fire with fire. It still seems like such a waste, though." For Inglis, the idea of pitting two strong enemies against each other instead of having to—instead of *getting* to—fight either was a crushing blow, even if the strategy was sound.

"Are you still complaining about that, Chris?" Rafinha teased. "C'mon, this is a great idea. It'll let us defend ourselves without having to commit any resources."

"You're right, but…"

Leone cupped her chin. "So even though magicite beasts don't care about borders at all, there are still people whose first thought is expanding theirs…"

Rafael nodded. "Yeah. It's a shame that humans still fight among themselves, even under the Prism Flow. This is meant to stop that, but… It still feels strange, relying on magicite beasts to do it."

The neighboring country, Venefic, had repeatedly attempted both incursions and full-scale invasions in the past. Tensions between nations still remained high, and Venefic was likely their greatest threat other than the magicite beasts. The main purpose of this airlift was to use the magicite beasts as a frontline of defense against Venefic's army. The plan came from Prince Wayne, who was quite a strategist in his own right.

"All right, Rani, Chris, Leone. This Flygear Port will be returning to the capital. You three can take it there. Ripple and I will stay behind to direct the airlift."

"Okay. Thanks, Rafael!" Rafinha smiled.

"Yes, thanks," Inglis said.

Leona bowed her head. "Thank you for everything, Rafael."

"Of course. Do your best at the knights' academy, you three. I'm looking forward to fighting alongside you someday." Rafael grinned at the girls.

"Hey, hey, Chrissy! You got a second?" Ripple took Inglis's arm and led her into an isolated corner of the Flygear Port, then whispered furtively. "It's you, right? You're the crazy girl Eris was talking about?"

"Oh, Eris mentioned me?"

"Yeah. But it was just between us hieral menaces, right?"

Inglis paused. "Thanks."

"Anyway. What do you really think of that there Prismer?"

"I think it's a pity it's being moved so far away."

"A-ha! ♪ You're not scared one bit, are ya? How about it? Think you could take it on?"

"I don't fight to *lose*."

"Listen, let's keep this between you and me, but I think you're gonna get your wish pretty soon now."

"What?! Really?! I knew I felt something from it, but..."

"Really-really. That big ol' guy ain't dead yet. He's just taking a little nap. I saw it for myself. Saw it for myself a long, long time ago."

Inglis gasped. "I'd heard hieral menaces were long-lived, but..."

"We sure are. I could well be your granny. So could Eris."

Inglis, of course, knew that she was old enough to have been *their* grandpa, if not many more generations back, even though they would never believe her if she said so.

"Anyway, we're just calling the Prismer dead to keep everyone's morale up, you know? If it's creating magicite beasts now, it's gotta be waking up. Better to get it away from any of the civvies while it's still groggy."

"Sounds great. Move it to somewhere where we can go all-out."

"I can see how hyped up you are!"

"Oh, extremely!"

"That's the stuff. ♪ Glad you're on board, Inglis. When that thing

## Chapter IX: Inglis, Age 15—The Rimebound Prismer

wakes up, you'll be the first to hear. So I'm gonna need you to do your best to get stronger until then."

"Understood. I'll be waiting."

"Looking forward to it. So, let's pinky promise!"

"Of course."

Before long, it was time to split ways.

"All right, everyone! I'll see you in the capital after I'm done!" Rafael said.

"Bye-bye! You cuties do your best, 'kay? See ya! ♪" Ripple said.

The pair climbed aboard their Flygear, and as it took off, Rafael's voice echoed from its cockpit. "We're off, then! New magicite beasts may appear at any time, so be on guard as we move!"

At Rafael's order, the Prismer began to recede into the distance.

Inglis stayed on the flight deck of the Flygear Port for a while, watching the Prismer shrink away, calling out to it from her heart. *Wake up soon, so we can have a good fight!*

"Well, it's time we returned to the capital!" the captain of the Flygear Port announced. As it picked up speed, Ahlemin soon sank under the horizon.

Leone watched, an intent look on her face. "Someday I shall return, holding my head high."

"That's right! You'll change their minds—I just know it!" Rafinha smiled.

Inglis nodded. "And we'll be helping out."

"Thanks, both of you."

And thus, Inglis and Rafinha's journey to the capital came to a close. Their first day at the knights' academy would arrive soon.

# Extra: The Talisman's Ward

Rafinha's jaw was half-slack as she took in the sights of the capital. "Wow, there sure are a lot of people here. Way different from Ymir."

"It sure is," Inglis said.

With a few days left before they were officially inducted into the knights' academy, the two were exploring the capital.

"Even the streets are wider. So many people, so many shops…"

"Rani, quit gawking like that. You look like a tourist."

Leone sighed at the mountains of snacks in the pair's arms. "I don't think Rafinha staring is the biggest problem here, to be honest. Even if her mouth wasn't hanging open, that mountain of food would attract more than enough attention."

Inglis and Rafinha had bought everything they saw that looked tasty. They were carrying so many things that it was hard to balance them all. That, surely, was far more gripping than any amazed expression could be.

Rafinha grinned. "Oh, that won't be any problem, Leone. Right, Chris?"

"Yep."

"It'll be gone soon," the two announced in unison.

"What?! But you've got so—"

In the blink of an eye, Inglis and Rafinha devoured their snacks, crunching and gobbling everything up.

"See? All gone!" Rafinha beamed.

"It was delicious." Inglis rubbed her stomach.

"You two really amaze me sometimes…" Leone, shocked, couldn't find any other words.

"All right, Chris, onto the next place! Their food looks tasty too!"

"Yeah. And we've still got money left."

"All right! I want to try every restaurant in this city!" Rafinha picked up her pace, starting to leave Inglis and Leone behind.

"Rafinha almost seems like…a little boy sometimes," Leone commented, pausing mid-sentence as she weighed her words.

"She's still young," Inglis said.

But that was one of her charms. To Inglis, Rafinha was practically the granddaughter she'd never had.

"Huh?" As Inglis watched Rafinha march forth, from the corner of her eye, she noticed a little girl glumly staring into a shop window. Her eyes were full of tears.

*What's going on here?*

"Hold on a second, Leone. You too, Rani," Inglis said to get their attention.

Rafinha was the first to speak to the girl. "What's wrong? You can tell me—I'll help out. What's your name?"

"Wow, she's fast," Leone said.

"That's Rani for you." Inglis walked next to her, a bit proud of how Rafinha had grown up.

The little girl sobbed between breaths. "I'm Ettie. This shop sells magicite charms. I saved up my allowance to buy one for daddy. He's going somewhere far away and I want him to stay safe, but…" She kept crying. "They're all sold out…"

Magicite was, as the name implied, a gemlike stone that grew on magicite beasts. However, only parts of their bodies were magicite, and those parts tended to fade away and crumble as the beast died. Only rarely did some stay intact as magicite. According to rumors, the wearer of a polished magicite pendant—or similar jewelry—wouldn't be attacked by magicite beasts. Since it was rare, dangerous to acquire, and said to be a safeguard against the beasts, it tended to be extremely pricey.

"Ettie, can you tell us how much they cost?" Leone asked gently.

"Um..." Ettie paused and then gave them a low number. This shop's charms were probably fake.

Still, that wasn't any real problem. Magicite itself was nothing more than an abandoned shell. It held no real power of its own. It couldn't compare to the power of a young girl's pure wishes—at least, people believed those wishes contained a special kind of strength.

"You're a good girl, Ettie. I bet your dad will be really proud of you just for trying." Rafinha patted the girl's head.

"But... I can't go home without one..."

"Hey, Rani, do you have any magicite?" Inglis would have given Ettie some if she'd had any on her, but they'd fought plenty of magicite beasts since leaving Ymir. Maybe Rafinha had picked some up along the way.

"Huh? Me?"

"Yeah. I don't have any, but I figured maybe you could give her some."

"Aha ha ha, well, ummm..."

"Really, Rani? If you have any, you should just give it to her. This isn't like you."

The more Inglis pushed, the more Rafinha resisted. Inglis found it all so strange. What was she hiding?

At the same time, Rin clambered into Rafinha's pocket.

"Eeek! W-W-W-Wait, Rin!"

Rin emerged, clutching a wooden box in her paws. It fell to the ground, and once the top popped off, it revealed an unpolished yellow chunk of magicite.

"Aha! I knew it! But why were you hiding that?"

"It... It's from back then—back when we were eight..."

"When we were eight?"

"Don't you remember that one time, Chris?"

Rafinha launched into a trip down memory lane.

◆◇◆

Seven years before, when Inglis and Rafinha were only eight years old, Inglis had visited Rafinha's room in the castle, only to find her pale in the face and sobbing.

"Rani? What's wrong?"

"Waaaaaah! Chris!" Rafinha immediately latched onto Inglis's arm.

"Whoa. What's wrong?"

"Um... You have to keep this a secret! Don't tell anyone!"

"Okay."

"I lost my warding talisman..."

"What?!"

The warding talisman was a magicite-decorated pendant that had been made for Rafinha when she was born. It was a tradition in Ymir to make a talisman from a piece of magicite found that year for newborns that would protect them from harm. When they turned fifteen, the talisman, its role complete, would be returned to the earth. It was a precious thing, normally kept safe and secure, but children were expected to wear it at birthday celebrations and other ceremonies—and Rafinha's birthday would be soon. She needed to have it.

"We should tell everyone so they can help—"

"No! If we do, they'll know it's gone! Mom and Dad will get really, really mad!"

"I guess, but..."

"Let's try to find it without them noticing! You'll help, right?"

"Okay..."

Inglis and Rafinha searched Rafinha's room, to no avail. Moving on, they tried Inglis's room and the nursery, but still they came up with nothing.

"It isn't anywhere," Inglis concluded.

"Wh-Wh-Wh-Wh-What do I do?! Wait, I know! What if I borrow yours, Chris?"

"They're different colors. I think people would be able to tell." Inglis quickly shot down Rafinha's plan. After all, her talisman was red, and Rafinha's was yellow.

"Maybe if we save up our allowances..."

"Magicite's pretty expensive. We probably wouldn't be able to afford it."

Rafinha sobbed.

"Maybe we should tell them what happened, and apolo—"

"No!" Rafinha angrily shook her head.

*I wonder what's up? I know the talisman is important, but Rani isn't usually this stubborn.* "But why? This isn't like you, Rani." Inglis patted her head to calm her down.

"Mom and Dad always tell me I should be more like Rafael or you! I don't want them to think I'm a bad girl!"

Inglis listened in silence. Rafinha was still a child, but children had their own worries. They had more to themselves than being cute. Rafinha's goal wasn't particularly admirable, but still, Inglis was inclined to help her. *I really do go too easy on her sometimes. But realizing it and being able to avoid it are two different things.*

"Okay, Rani. I understand. I'll try to do something, so—"

"Really?! Do you have any ideas?!"

"Yeah. It'll be fine, don't worry. But it's getting late. You should head back to the castle."

"Okay! Thanks, Chris!"

Inglis walked with Rafinha back to the castle. "Don't worry, okay? Anyway, goodnight."

"Yeah! Goodnight, Chris!" Rafinha soon fell into a peaceful sleep, reassured by Inglis's words.

The next morning, Irina, half-panicked, shook her daughter awake. "Rafinha... Rafinha! Sorry, honey, but you need to get up!"

Rafinha yawned. "What, Mom?"

"Do you know where Chris went? She walked you back to the castle yesterday, right?"

"Yeah."

"Did she say anything to you? We haven't been able to find her anywhere since last night."

"Whaaaat?! Chris is gone?"

"Please, please, tell me if she said anything at all unusual! I don't know where a center of attention like that could have disappeared to!"

"Umm... I dunno..." Rafinha shook her head. She was too afraid of what would happen if she told the truth.

As Irina questioned her, the hubbub spread. Some knights organized a search party, as others, and the merchants, were asked if they'd seen the Prism Flow recently.

Wherever Inglis had gone, it wasn't in Ymir. A search party combed the surrounding countryside, but as the sun set, they called off their efforts for the day. Rafinha was beside herself with worry, and thought she'd be up all night, unable to sleep.

*Tap, tap. Tap, tap.*

There was someone just outside her window. As she peeked out nervously, she saw what seemed to be a light-haired wisp floating there—but it was Inglis, perched neatly but precariously on her third-story windowsill.

"Ah! Chris! Are you okay?!" Rafinha immediately swept the window open.

"Shhh! Quiet down or I'll get caught."

"Okay..." Rafinha sobbed. "You're back... I'm so happy you're back."

Inglis smiled at her. "Yeah. I'm back, Rani. And I found a replacement piece of magicite." It was the same vivid yellow as the old talisman. Inglis had found the Prism Flow, hunted a magicite beast, and returned with its magicite.

It was rare for magicite beasts to leave behind magicite at all.

Hunting a specific color within that was a daunting task indeed. Inglis had wanted to finish it overnight, but even she had needed a whole day.

"I'm a little bit late. They'd be mad at me if I came back with a magicite stone, so I wanted to give it to you as soon as I could."

"Thanks, Chris!"

"This way, they'll never find out. Anyway, I'm going home."

"Okay!" After a pause, Rafinha caught Inglis's sleeve. "Wait, Chris!"

"What's wrong?"

"This is my fault! I don't want it to be my fault the grownups are mad at you! So even though I shouldn't have asked you to hide it, I'll tell them everything and apologize!"

"I guess. Yeah, that's probably for the best. But I was bad too, so I'll apologize with you."

"Okay!"

And thus, the two came clean to their families.

The two daughters: "We're so sorry!"

The two fathers: "What were you thinking?!"

The two mothers: "Honey, please calm down!"

In the end, Inglis and Rafinha were sent to sit in the storeroom overnight to think about what they'd done.

*Bonk!*

As Rafinha rambled around the room, she bumped into a shelf. "Ah! There it is!"

Rafinha's warding talisman was in plain view.

"What's it doing here?" Inglis asked.

"I-I guess I took it off because it was getting in my way while I was looking around here?"

"All the things you could be doing, and you decided to clamber around a storeroom? You're such a tomboy sometimes, Rani."

"Sorry, Chris…"

"Well. I guess we don't need this magicite anymore."

"That's not true! You went out and got it just for me! I'm keeping it for the rest of my life!" Rafinha smiled as she tightly gripped the magicite—the one that Inglis had found just for her.

◆◇◆

Inglis clapped her hands together as the memories came flooding back. "Oh! The magicite from then? You didn't bury it with your talisman?"

"Of course not! I said I'd cherish this for the rest of my life!"

"Then what do we do? That's the only magicite..." Inglis couldn't think of any other way to help Ettie.

"Wait," Leone cut in. "It sounds like that magicite's pretty important to you two. It's important to be kind to other people, but your own memories are important too." Then she pulled a purple piece of magicite from her pocket. "Here, Ettie. You can have this."

"Th-Thanks so much, lady!" Ettie said excitedly.

"Don't worry about it. Now, I want you to take good care of your dad, okay?"

"Yeah! Thanks again, lady! Goodbye!" Ettie waved and ran off home.

Rafinha brushed her palm across her brow in relief. "You're a lifesaver, Leone! I was really in a bind."

Inglis nodded. "Yeah, thanks. You're sure you're okay with this, though?"

"Yeah. I picked it up off a magicite beast—that's all. But I'm glad I did." Leone grinned.

"It feels great to do some good! I bet it'll make the food even tastier! Let's go, Chris!" Rafinha warmly tugged at Inglis's arm, closer to her than ever.

# Afterword

First, thank you very much for picking up this book! This wraps up the first volume of *Reborn to Master the Blade: From Hero-King to Extraordinary Squire ♀*. What did you think?

On a personal note, it seems like this is about my twentieth book. Honestly, I'm a bit amazed at how far I've come. When I first started writing, I'd hoped I could strike it big and retire off the money, but somehow, I'm still down here in the salt mines. Life is cruel. It wasn't supposed to be like this! And I've been sick all year, yet somehow I managed to power through.

It's fun to write light novels, though, so I want to get myself back into shape to keep going. There are still so many stories I want to tell, so many things I want to try—though this was pretty experimental and an adventure in its own right.

For starters, it's the first time I've decided to write a female protagonist (even if, in her own head, Inglis still thinks of herself as the old hero-king, just gender-bent). I always used to assume that my protagonists would be guys, so writing this—having written this—is a big change. I need to get invested in the story before I can write it, and it was thanks to sitting down with the kids to watch *PreC\*re* and playing games with them that I really opened my eyes to writing this story.

Things like the magicite beasts, Highland, and hieral menaces are all ideas I've had bouncing around my head since my first book, so there are a lot of pretty serious scenes and concepts. But Inglis, that lovable gender-bent meathead, managed to smash her way right through all the doom and gloom. I don't think I've ever felt like this before. It's refreshing. I can't wait to see how she mauls all the gritty ideas I was taking seriously.

There are a bunch of scenes I've had floating around in my head since I started putting the web novel online. I hope to someday fit them all into a book. This series is even getting a manga version, so with that on the way, somehow… Somehow I'll do it! It's the first time I've ever been adapted, so I'm really hyped! It'll be starting in *Comic Fire* soon, so check it out!

Finally, I'd like to thank my editor N, the illustrator Nagu, and everyone involved with this project for all their hard work. Just looking at the cover of this volume has me fired up to write more. Thank you so much! I can't wait to see what the next cover will be.

See you then!

# HEY ///////
▶ **HAVE YOU HEARD OF J-Novel Club?**

It's the digital publishing company that brings you the latest novels and manga from Japan!

Subscribe today at

▶▶▶ **j-novel.club** ◀◀◀

and read the latest volumes as they're translated, or become a premium member to get a *FREE* ebook every month!

---

Check Out The Latest Volume Of
**Reborn to Master the Blade:
From Hero-King to Extraordinary Squire** ♀

---

Plus Our Other Hit Series Like:

- Min-Maxing My TRPG Build in Another World
- Campfire Cooking in Another World with My Absurd Skill
- I Shall Survive Using Potions!
- Black Summoner
- Knight's & Magic
- My Quiet Blacksmith Life in Another World

- The Invincible Little Lady
- The Retired Demon of the Maxed-Out Village
- Now I'm a Demon Lord! Happily Ever After with Monster Girls in My Dungeon
- Back to the Battlefield: The Veteran Heroes Return to the Fray!

...and many more!

*In Another World With My Smartphone, Illustration © Eiji Usatsuka*  *Arifureta: From Commonplace to World's Strongest, Illustration © Takayaki*